stealing BASES

stealing BASES

a novel by

keri mikulski

Stealing Bases

RAZORBILL

Published by the Penguin Group
Penguin Young Readers Group
345 Hudson Street, New York, New York 10014, U.S.A.
Penguin Group (USA) Inc., 375 Hudson Street, New York, New York 10014, U.S.A.
Penguin Group (Canada), 90 Eglinton Avenue East, Suite 700, Toronto, Ontario, Canada M4P 2Y3 (a division of Pearson Penguin Canada Inc.)
Penguin Books Ltd, 80 Strand, London WC2R 0RL, England
Penguin Ireland, 25 St Stephen's Green, Dublin 2, Ireland (a division of Penguin Books Ltd)
Penguin Group (Australia), 250 Camberwell Road, Camberwell, Victoria 3124, Australia (a division of Pearson Australia Group Pty Ltd)
Penguin Books India Pvt Ltd, 11 Community Centre, Panchsheel Park, New Delhi – 110 017, India
Penguin Group (NZ), 67 Apollo Drive, Mairangi Bay, Auckland 1311, New Zealand (a division of Pearson New Zealand Ltd)
Penguin Books (South Africa) (Pty) Ltd, 24 Sturdee Avenue, Rosebank, Johannesburg 2196, South Africa

Penguin Books Ltd, Registered Offices: 80 Strand, London WC2R 0RL, England

10 9 8 7 6 5 4 3 2 1
ISBN: 978-159514-393-8

Series created by Jane Schonberger

Library of Congress Cataloging-in-Publication Data is available

Printed in the United States of America

*pretty*TOUGH Novels:

PRETTYTOUGH

PLAYING WITH THE BOYS

HEAD GAMES

STEALING BASES

For Sydney and Sabrina

one

From this day forward, I, Kylie Elizabeth Collins, will not freak out at any more girls who touch, talk to, wink at, brush up against, sit next to, cheer for, check out, or proclaim their undying love for my ex-boyfriend, Beachwood Academy basketball star Zachary Michael Murphy.

Wait a second. Scratch check out. And touch. And definitely the one about proclaiming their undying love. That's just wrong. I mean, Zachary and I were together for a really long time. Were these girls born without hearts?

At least I'm trying here. I want to change my crazy-Kylie rep and begin the spring season with a brand-new attitude. No more freaking out. No more psychotic behavior. And definitely no more back and forth with my ex. Softball season is here. It's time to get serious.

Meet the new Kylie Collins.

"Cutting down the net was the best part of three-peating," our senior captain, Tamika, recalls as my B-Dub basketball buds and I wait in line for cupcakes at Sprinkles.

"What? Are we seriously reliving our glory days? Basketball season has been over for months already." My lip-gloss-aholic best friend, fellow junior Missy Adams, rolls her eyes.

My teammates laugh.

I don't.

Although I do agree with Missy, basketball season seems like a distant memory after everything I've been going through lately. A few months ago, my entire world came crashing down when my parents split up. Toss in my mom moving cross-country to work in New York City, my dad's obsession with "living a balanced lifestyle," this stupid "three-B" list of all the girls the guys on the basketball team hooked up with, and some serious Zachary-cheating rumors, and that's enough to drive any girl crazy. And I'm not one to keep emotions on the down low. So, needless to say, I've been a wee bit stressed.

I force a smile and stare at my shiny, silver basketball championship ring. At least I still have sports.

Attending Beachwood Academy, an elite private school in Malibu, is tough enough, but snagging a three-peat was close to impossible. But we B-Dub girls did it. And to congratulate us, our headmaster presented the team with gorgeous sapphire rings at a lunch reception held in our honor at the Beachwood Country Club. Which explains why I'm now busy reminiscing instead of squeezing in some extra pitching practice before tomorrow's tryouts.

Not that I'm in danger of not making the cut this year . . .

My gaze drifts from my ring to my red velvet cupcake, my mouth watering at the thick cream cheese icing. What a perfect way to begin my new life the day before my fave season—softball—officially kicks off. What could be better than spending the day with my stunning new ring, my favorite dessert of all time, and my best buds?

"I can't believe I'll never play another high school basketball game again," Tamika laments, pulling on the strings of her USC hoodie.

"But you'll be playing college ball next year, which is way better," Eva, a fellow junior, adds. She removes a white iPod bud from her ear. "Uh-huh. Uh-huh. Uh-huh," she sings, bobbing her head to the Trojan fight song.

Everyone laughs except me.

I'm too busy thinking about how to become the next Tamika to bother faking a laugh. Like Tamika, I'm determined to one day be recruited by a Division I school. Only it'll be for softball. And I'll be crosstown in UCLA's blue and gold.

Not that UCLA knows I exist yet. But I'm planning on fixing that with bi-weekly emails, a professionally produced highlight reel, and recruitment packages to all the coaches and assistants. Don't ever say that I'm not willing to put in the work. Now I just have to put Zachary and the three-B list behind me.

"What I still can't believe is that the guys actually competed against each other to see how many girls they could hook up with. That was horrible. . . ." Abby, a freshman JV starter and occasional varsity sub, announces.

Horrible? I admit, the three-B list sucked, but I wouldn't call a

bunch of boys acting like dogs "horrible." That's normal. What's horrible is that I'm living in my ex-boyfriend Zachary Murphy's guesthouse right now because my dad refuses my mom's alimony and claims our old house had bad karma.

"Seriously," Zoe, Zachary's younger sister, a freshed-face frosh, says. She nudges her best friend Abby's arm. "Can I have a piece?" Zoe asks, pointing to Abby's cupcake. I stare at her Abercrombie tee and think about the Christmas morning that I gave it to her. Zoe is the only person here who knows where I'm really living: a cottage in her backyard. My hand goes to the silver heart charm hanging around my neck, a present from Zachary that same Christmas morning.

"Only at B-Dub. Tamika rolls her eyes behind her sunglasses.

Freshman Taylor Thomas glances up at me, and I untangle a piece of long, blonde hair from the clasp of my necklace. I feel like she's silently telling me to ditch the Tiffany open-heart pendant. But it's not like she even knows how I got it. Just because she had a quick fling with my boyfriend, ahem, ex-boyfriend, doesn't give her insider info. She sees me glowering at her and looks back down at her strawberry cupcake.

Sensing the tension, Missy steps in to save me from myself. "So, what have you been up to since the season ended, Tay?" Missy asks.

"Oh, not much." Taylor smiles, looking relieved that someone rescued her from my silent wrath.

"Not much?" Hannah Montgomery intervenes, gazing at

her BFF Taylor with her crystal-blue eyes. "You mean since you killed it as a model in the Spring Fashion Show and kissed Matt Moore in front of the whole school?"

How did Taylor think she had the right to bring Hannah today? It's not like Missy or I asked for a freshman parade.

Taylor squirms in her wrought-iron chair and turns the exact same color as her strawberry cupcake. "Well, you know . . . I . . ."

Hannah shakes her head in mock disapproval and then looks at the rest of us. "I didn't know Taylor had it in her."

"Believe me, Taylor has it in her." I laugh, breaking a piece of cupcake in between my fingers. "JK," I add for good measure, even though I don't really mean it.

"Kylie. Remember our deal," Tamika reminds me, holding up three fingers. "Basketball Before Boys."

"I was just kidding," I say, shoving the piece of pure decadence into my mouth. "And anyway, it's not like it's basketball season anymore. So, no more boy bans. We won the championship already, remember?"

Tamika rolls her eyes. It's clear that I'm not the only one who's having a hard time letting last season go.

"Subject change *numero deux*," Missy announces. She gives me a look like *I-know-what-you're-going-through* as I shove another piece of cupcake into my mouth.

I definitely wouldn't call Missy Zachary's number-one fan, but she's the only one who pseudo-gets what I'm going through—she's had boyfriend troubles of her own.

Jessica steps in. "Are you excited for all the college scouts coming to our softball games, Ky?" she asks, her almond eyes wide. Jessica is the only one of these girls who has played with me on both my basketball and softball teams.

I'm tempted to say, "Hells yeah! I'm gonna tear it up there and UCLA is going to be *dying* to recruit me." But I don't think that will go over too well. Or really work for my plan: *Attitude—Take Two.* So I just say, "I guess," which is the understatement of the century.

Missy looks at me like I'm a moron not to toot my own horn. "Uh, hello, you're amazing!" she exclaims. "You're like the best pitcher Beachwood's ever had."

"Ditto," Eva adds.

"Still working on the rise ball with Coach Malone," I add. Playing for the American Softball Association, or ASA, on the side is a constant reminder of how much work I have to do. Although I *am* pretty amazing at both pitcher and second base (if I do say so myself), I'm far from the best and I'm definitely not a power pitcher. And if I want UCLA to pay attention to me, I'll have to increase my speed and nail the rise ball. And quickly.

"If anyone can do it, you can," Taylor adds.

I just ignore her.

Jessica doesn't. "Yeah," she chimes in, licking icing off her finger. "Remember the screwball last year? You thought you'd never nail it and now it's your go-to pitch."

I think back to last year and how hard I worked on my

screwball. And that's when another memory of Zachary hits me . . . the zillionth one today. Night after night at the field with him dodging my screwballs as he played catcher for me until I gained control of the pitch. *And now* . . . I bite my bottom lip.

"By the way, um . . . did you guys hear what weekend junior prom falls on this year?" Abby's eyes scan the group.

"Prom is in April, like always, right?" Missy asks, checking her lips in her compact.

"Yeah, but it's the same day as the Desert Invitational!" Abby continues, the pitch of her voice heightening. "I heard it at one of our student council meetings with Ms. Sealer. And since I'm hoping to make JV softball this year . . ."

Jessica juts out her bottom lip. "I thought Ms. Sealer said she was going to try to avoid a sports conflict."

Jessica's a soph—it's not like she could possibly care about prom as much as I do. The only reason she'd be going to the junior prom is because of her boyfriend Colin. She's not even eligible for prom princess.

"Not that it matters to me, but I'm sure the boys are clear," Tamika says, rolling her eyes.

"Always," Missy adds, dabbing her lips with the wand.

My mind starts to reel with how I'm never going to live my dream—well, my mom's dream—of being named prom princess, just like her, when I realize something.

"Beachwood Academy Softball hasn't been invited to the Desert Invitational in like ten years," I announce. "What are you guys worried about? We're never going to be good enough to snag an invitation."

"You never know. We're pretty stacked with Nyla at short and you on the mound," Jessica says, wiping her mouth with a Sprinkles napkin.

"Guess it's a good thing no junior is going to invite me—I can't imagine playing a tournament game the same day as prom," Abby admits.

And no Zachary to invite me . . . I gulp and slide the cardboard cupcake box across the wrought-iron table.

"Call the ambulance. Kylie Collins just passed up a red velvet cupcake," Eva jokes, elbowing me playfully.

"Ha ha," I mock my teammates. If only I opened up. If only I told them that I can't imagine prom without Zachary, that I'm dying to be named prom princess, that I'm hoping it all magically comes together so that my mom sees me following in her footsteps and decides to visit on a regular basis. Maybe then they would realize why I'm such a mess. But the last thing I need is everyone knowing my business. Mom always says: *Never show anyone your weakness or they'll use it against you.*

"So, Ky, what are you going to do this year when you make prom court and have to pitch at the Desert Invitational the same day?" Jessica asks, sipping from her straw.

"Yeah, sure," I say. "Ending the season with a winning record is a maybe, but the Desert Invitational is tough. . ."

I continue, "And besides, Missy is going to be the one who you're all bowing down to."

"Yeah, only if you're too busy flirting with the college coaches to make it to the ballroom," Missy answers, doing her best impression of me waving at scouts.

"Isn't prom . . ." Hannah scrunches her nose. "Like two months away?"

"Six weeks," Taylor says, matter-of-factly.

"Someone is counting down . . ." Tamika says, adjusting her ponytail.

"Counting down to going with Matt . . ." Eva jokes.

Taylor giggles and gives Hannah a little nudge. "Counting down to wearing the gorgeous Banana Fad dress Hannah's designing."

Gag.

"Aw . . ." Hannah stops playing with the bottle cap necklace she insists on wearing and gives Taylor a quasi-hug.

"It's not just my dress that I can't wait for. It's all the pre-prom prep!" Jessica announces, bouncing in her seat.

"I know! Now I don't have to justify it to my mom when I get a mani-pedi, facial, and massage all in one week!" Missy's eyes widen.

"Miss, don't forget about your hair . . ." I reply. I can't resist indulging in Missy's excitement.

"Ohmigod, my hair!" she exclaims.

"And what about *your* dress?" I continue.

"My dress . . . I . . ." Missy sputters.

"You didn't tell her?" Hannah asks, disbelievingly.

"I didn't have a chance . . . I . . ."

"You didn't tell me what?" I ask, my eyes demanding an immediate answer.

Missy just stares at me guiltily.

I glare back. *What could Hannah possibly know about Missy that I don't?*

"Missy and I . . . We're in business together. Fashion design," Hannah announces.

"You're working?" I screech. "With Hannah?"

Missy stands up and tosses the empty box into the trash can. As she passes by me, she mumbles a "yeah."

"Yeah, we're partners. And we're counting on prom to be our entry into the big time," Hannah explains, a glob of frosting smeared across her lower left cheek.

Ew.

"Hannah tracked me down a few weeks ago." Missy plops back down in the seat next to me. "I find the clients, Hannah designs. That's all. . . ." Then, leaning over, she whispers in my ear, "It's for college . . . More later." Missy looks at me for confirmation that this is okay.

It's not.

I stare blankly back. Apparently, I'm not the only one with secrets.

Taylor interjects. "I'm so, so excited for you guys! I knew Hannah was planning on designing my prom dress, but when

I found out a couple weeks ago that it's the first dress from your collective new line . . . That's just so much better!"

A couple weeks ago? Wait. Where have I been? How long have they been hanging out?

"Thanks, Tay. I know we'll dazzle you with our impressive skills," Missy replies.

"So, who's in besides Taylor?" Hannah licks the frosting off her cheek.

Gross.

"I am!" Tamika claps. "I'd love to have a one-of-a-kind dress for senior prom."

"Me too!" Jessica announces. "I've wanted a Banana Fad dress ever since Hannah rocked the Spring Fashion Show.

"Count me in. You know how I love original style. And so does Xavier," Eva adds, her eyes glimmering with satisfaction at the mention of her DJ boyfriend.

Seven pairs of eyes descend on me.

For a moment, I just look pleadingly at Missy. Doesn't she remember how much prom means to me? And what a sore subject it is? Sure, we haven't talked about how my mom was prom princess in a while. But how could she forget that I always wanted to go mother-daughter shopping? And how could she possibly overlook that my mom is three thousand miles away?

Missy's eyes are wide. She's waiting for my answer just like the rest of them. So I give them a classic Kylie: "Prom's too important to leave to an amateur. . . . No offense." I look at Hannah, then Missy.

They all sigh in disgust.

But I can't bring myself to tell them the truth—that prom shopping may be the only way I'll get my mom to come home for a weekend. Besides, if Missy, who I thought was my best friend, can't see past her fashion design "business" and her perfect Stepford family to understand what I'm going through, then none of them can. I'm all alone.

two

"Welcome, Wildcats," Coach Kate announces, greeting us each individually as we enter the Beachwood Academy Field House the next day.

"Hey, Coach!" I say, beaming. I've adored Coach Kate ever since she spotted me on the Beachwood Middle School mound five years ago.

"Hello, Kylie," Coach says, glancing at me. "How's it going with Coach Malone?"

"Amazing. You should see my rise ball!" I say. And then I kick myself for saying it. My rise ball isn't exactly stellar at the moment.

Coach, decked out in her signature Beachwood attire, smiles. "Great." She turns back to greeting girls I don't recognize.

A briny scent of salt from the nearby shore fills the field house air as I scan the familiar and not so familiar faces. The freshmen glance sideways at me as we inconspicuously try to size each other up. They avert their gaze the second they see me notice them. *If Zachary so much as sank his claws into another freshman girl, I'm going to . . .*

"Kylie!" my ASA teammate Chloe, a freshman who's expected to make varsity this year, jogs over to me, interrupting my ill-advised thoughts of vengeance. Her curly blonde ponytail swings back and forth as she bounces in her way-too-tiny cotton shorts and tee. "Can you believe we're back already?"

Great. The first girl I have to see is Chloe.

"Yeah," I say, scanning the team room in an attempt to keep myself from looking at Chloe. Word is, Chloe made out with Zachary while I was away skiing at Telluride over Christmas break last year. Although the two of them vehemently denied the hookup, I figure ignoring Chloe can't hurt.

"Hey, Zoe," I call out. I push my way toward my quasi-roommate, giving Chloe the brush-off. When I reach her, I give her skinny elbow a quick squeeze. She drops the catcher's mitt she was busy playing with to her side and looks up at me with deep brown eyes. Her mouth breaks into a grin, showing off two dimples.

And that's when the resemblance to Zachary hits me. I quickly pull my hand back. Even though Zoe and I practically grew up together, it's hard to look at her without thinking of her brother. Even if we did just finish our first basketball season together.

"Hey, Ky." Zoe moves toward me, giving me a hug. As much as I love Zoe, it's all I can do to stop myself from running in the opposite direction when the Zachary memories strike.

"There you are!" Jessica squeezes in next to Zoe. She grabs my hands and starts to jump up and down. "It's time for softball season!" She beams.

"The *best* season." I wink.

"Ky!" Phoenix, our third baseman, jogs from the back of the pack to join us. "How's it going?" She eyes me up and down like she's scoping out another piece of jewelry to add to her enormous collection.

"Amazing," I say, feeling the wave of excitement in the room.

"Nice highlights." She touches a honey-blonde wave.

"Thanks, I try," I reply.

Phoenix waves to Nyla, our returning shortstop and future Florida Gator. "Nyla!" she shouts.

Nyla's face lights up. She waves back. "Phoenix! Ky!" Then she maneuvers through the team room to join us. "What's up, girls?" she exclaims, pushing up the sleeves of her Gators Softball hoodie.

"Uh, our upcoming season," I answer, too busy picturing myself walking into the UCLA team room to bother being my usual sarcastic self.

When I look around, I notice that we're surrounded by girls in ASA tees and summer club hoodies eavesdropping on our conversation.

I ignore them and lean in closer to my friends, whispering, "Have you guys noticed that we've been ambushed by freshmen?"

"Yeah, guess they think that if they hang out with us, they might just make the team." Phoenix giggles.

"Like it's that easy," Nyla replies.

Zoe just shakes her head. After being friends with me for me so long, she knows to take all this anti-frosh talk in stride.

Out of the corner of my eye, I see a familiar blur of brunette hair. A hand waves to us frantically in the distance. "Uh-oh, guys. I think one of us is trapped," I say. I reach my hand out, through the throng of nervous girls, and pull my friend Emily in.

By the time Emily is standing next to us, she's shaking her head. "Seriously. Who do these girls think they are? I don't remember being like this my first year," she announces as soon as she's checked to make sure that she didn't lose anything in all the commotion.

"That's what Kylie was thinking." Zoe giggles.

Emily turns to Zoe. "And you are?" she asks.

I step in before Zoe can answer. "She's your counterpart—hoping to be JV catcher. She's also Zachary's little sister."

Emily makes an O with her mouth. Before she can figure out how to respond to that bombshell, Coach Kate calls the assembly to order.

"Okay, everyone," Coach Kate shouts. "It's time to get started."

I take my seat on the first bench, along with the rest of the returning varsity team. Zoe squeezes in next to me, motioning for "Abs" to join us.

Flanked by her assistant coaches, Coach Kate scans the hopefuls. She pulls an Expo marker off the shelf of the huge whiteboard behind her. "The coaches and I are very excited about this upcoming season," she says, twirling the marker. "Looking out at the room, I see a lot of great talent. In fact, the other coaches and I are convinced this is our year—the year that will go down in Beachwood Softball history."

A few girls nervously clap and glance around.

"And that is why . . ." Coach pauses, and for one second I wonder if she forgot the rest of her speech.

Phoenix takes this opportunity to lean over and whisper, "Nice necklace."

I look down and realize that I've been mindlessly playing with my heart pendant ever since I sat down. "Thanks," I reply. I'm considering whether to tell her that it was a present from Zachary when I notice the room's gone quiet. I look back up.

Coach Kate is glancing uncomfortably at the assistant coaches. It must dawn on her that she's freaking us all out because she finally turns back to us. "As many of you know, I was brought on three years ago to revive this program to the powerhouse it once was." Coach adjusts her royal-blue BW visor. "In fact, Beachwood hasn't had a winning season in ten years. Last year, we went ten and twelve, coming close. But we lost our concentration at the end of the season." She raises her eyebrows as she looks at me.

Clearly, she didn't forget how I blew our final game of the

season because I was so exhausted from staying up all night, spying on Zachary. (I was worried something was going on between him and Susie Tabler. There wasn't.)

I force myself to move past this memory and try to focus on what Coach Kate is saying.

"This is a must-win year for us," Coach continues, clicking the marker cap, "since enrollment at Beachwood is dependent on our successful sports programs and top-notch academics. . . ." She takes a deep breath, steadying herself. Then, in a rush, she blurts out the big news. "I was given three years to turn this program around. This year is my third year. If we don't do something to show the Board of Trustees that we're back from our slump, the Beachwood Academy Softball program will be demoted to intramural status."

What? Did I hear Coach correctly? An intramural schedule? Why?

A few girls look like they're going to faint.

"Normally I wouldn't disclose this kind of administrative information. But I think it's imperative for everyone on the team to know their positions aren't safe." She pauses and then adds insult to injury. "I don't care whether you've played for me before or this is your first tryout. This season is a clean slate. Everyone has an equal shot of making the team."

"What?" A couple of girls gasp.

"That's not fair!" Emily squeals.

"Yes, you're right. It's not fair. But I'm not in control of these types of executive decisions, and I have to do what I can to make sure that we play at the highest level possible. Beachwood Academy Softball's future is on the line."

"This is crazy!" I shout.

"They can't do this," Phoenix spouts.

"Unfortunately, yes, they can. As some of you know, the lacrosse team was demoted to intramural status just two years ago. And they *still* haven't been reinstated to the inter-scholastic league. And of course, you all remember when the International Olympic Committee dropped softball from the Olympics. Let's not let that happen to our softball team here." Coach Kate tenses her mouth.

I gulp.

Coach soldiers on. "This isn't the time to give up. Beach-wood Academy Softball players are fighters. We're tough. And we're starting now. Today. We're not waiting around for a championship banner. We're going to meet the Board of Trustees' expectations *way* before the end of the season. We're not going to allow this to be Beachwood Softball's last year. We're going to bring home a Desert Invitational tournament banner in April!"

A couple of girls clap. Most of us just nervously look around the room. Yesterday's conversation at Sprinkles registers some-where in the deep dark recesses of my brain (as does the fact that Santo Bay has won the last two Desert Invitationals).

"Now, moving on to today's practice. This afternoon we'll just be getting to know each other. The assistant coaches and I won't begin formally evaluating you until tomorrow."

I take a deep breath and try to tell myself that none of this applies to me. Formal evaluation or not: that spot on the mound is mine. Sure, I slacked off after my parents' split, but I'm the returning two-year starting pitcher and I've been batting second in the lineup since the middle of my freshman year. Plus, I constantly practice with my ASA team—both as a pitcher and at second base—and I've been working hard this summer with Coach Malone, my pitching instructor, to master the one ingredient missing from my pitching arsenal: the rise ball.

Coach continues, "After we're done with the evaluation, we'll post the ten varsity starters, a backup pitcher, and four substitutes. Below that, we'll post the twelve of you who made junior varsity. The roster should be up on Wednesday after school."

Coach takes a moment for us to let this all sink in. She's certainly going for the *I-am-the-boss* mantra this year. If I was a newbie, I'd definitely be nervous.

Once she senses we've all had a chance to digest this information, she exclaims, "Let's get started!" Then she tosses the marker back on the whiteboard shelf and charges toward the door.

Zoe looks up at me. "I guess varsity is a long shot this year."

"Don't be ridiculous," I say, shrugging.

"Do you think we'll all be replaced?" Phoenix pulls out her batting glove and slides it onto her hand.

"Doubtful," I say, adjusting my ponytail. Then I grab Zoe's arm. Even if she is Zachary's sister, it's my job to take care of her. I pull her behind me and out the door.

I don't care what Coach Kate says. Nothing is going to get in my way this year. UCLA, here I come.

three

"Can you believe that?" Zoe asks as I pull her out of the field house. "I thought stuff like that didn't happen at B-Dub. Zach said—"

"Don't worry. It won't." I cut her off at the mention of her brother. "At least not if I have anything to do with it." I put my hand on Zoe's shoulder. "I promise I'll—"

"Kylie!" Before I can finish promising anything, Coach Kate calls me over to the pitching cage. "Hey, Kylie, I forgot to ask you—I'm attending a coach's clinic this summer, and we're allowed to bring two players from the team. Would you like to go?"

"Sure," I say, leaving out the implicit *who wouldn't?* Instead, I opt for the seasoned pro approach. "Will it be just like last year's?"

"Not quite. This year the focus is more on mental conditioning, rather than on skill-based drills."

"Oh . . ." I pause. "Perfect."

"I was hoping you'd be up for it." She smiles. "And, before I forget, I'd like to introduce you to someone."

I look around for my freaked-out freshman partner. Coach

is known for pairing up veterans with rookies. *Gotta love the first day of practice.*

A tiny girl, clad in an Orange County Crush ASA tee and tie-dyed socks, steps next to Coach. Her auburn hair is held back tight in a ponytail and a Jennie-Finch-inspired sparkly headband sits across the crown of her head.

I stare at the girl. I would know those freckles anywhere. What is *she* doing here? *She* doesn't go to Beachwood.

"Hey, I'm Amber," she says, holding out her hand. "Amber McDonald."

"I know who you are. I remember you from ASA," I say. An image of me standing inside the batter's box while three of the most powerful pitches I've ever seen hurtle past flashes before my eyes.

"Really?" she asks.

"Yeah, you struck m—uh, my teammate out three times."

"Oh, I hope I didn't embarrass her," Amber replies.

I look at her face for any hint of sarcasm. There isn't a sign to be found.

Coach takes this as a sign that we're a match made in heaven. "I'm so glad you girls are already acquainted! Kylie, I'd like you to show Amber the ropes," she says, distracted by her clipboard. "You'll be working together during the tryouts."

Great.

Coach walks away to join her assistants.

Okay. *Breathe.* So what if Amber's one of the best pitchers

in Southern California? So what if she's a junior like me? So what if she's gotten tons of press and won countless honors? I'm *going* to go D-I at UCLA and no transfer student is going to steal my spot.

I take a deep breath, feeling my lungs coil up. "Since I didn't have a chance to introduce myself last summer—I'm Kylie. Kylie Collins."

"It's great to meet you." She smiles and points to my pink-and-white Under Armour softball bag. "Love your bag."

"Thanks," I reply, not bothering to acknowledge that the bag is a year-old birthday gift from my mom. I force myself to give her an equally sweet response. "It's great to meet you in person too." I smile. I can do this. I can be nice to her for one measly practice. *And then I'll crush her . . .*

Amber follows me to the fenced-in pitching cage. My first instinct is to let the gate swing in her face, but I hold it open for her, pushing away the memories of me and Zachary practicing in this very spot.

"Thanks," Amber says, smiling widely enough to show off her shiny, white teeth.

I walk out toward the far side of the cage and grab a yellow softball from the bucket resting next to the pitching rubber. She can't be *that* amazing. She probably just got lucky against us last year.

I grip the ball, feeling for the familiar seams. My hand automatically assumes the C-grip. It's as if my hand has decided that I'm going to throw a fastball before my brain's had time to process.

At first, Amber and I throw in silence. I seriously can't think of anything to say to her. All that comes to mind is her stats, and it's not like I want to admit that I've combed through them obsessively ever since our last game together.

"So . . ." Amber looks around and tosses the ball back to me overhand. She's smiling, of course. "What pitching coach do you work with?"

"Coach Malone," I say, tossing the ball back to her. I shove my glove between my knees and stretch out my right arm.

"I used to work with Malone years ago." She catches my toss.

I wince. *If she were anyone else, I'd assume she means that Coach Malone wasn't good enough to stick with.*

"So, how long have you . . ." She begins to toss the ball back, but stops herself when she realizes I'm stretching and not ready to catch her ball. But not before the ball tumbles out of her hand toward me. "Oh my God . . ." Her face flushes and she jogs toward the ball. "I'm so sorry."

"No, really it's okay." I shake out my hand. The ball rolls a few feet ahead of me. "I'll get it."

"No, I'll . . ."

She's about to jog toward the ball when I cut her off, sprinting after it.

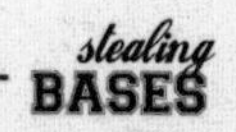

Seeing that I have the situation under control, Amber stops mid-stride and returns to the pitching cage. "I should have been paying better attention."

"Here," I say, placing the ball into her glove. She *should* be paying better attention.

She takes one look at the ball and hands it back to me. Then she walks toward her bag and pulls out two water bottles. "I brought an extra one. Here you go." She holds out an unopened bottle.

Ugh, she really is genuinely nice. Gag me with a bat.

"I'm okay," I say, snapping the ball into my glove with my wrist.

"If you're sure . . ." Amber takes a sip and sets up on the mound.

"So, why are you here?" I ask, bluntly. I mean, it had to be said eventually.

"Oh . . ." She continues to smile. "My parents divorced this summer."

Ouch. A divorce. I know about those. I can't possibly torture her now.

"That sucks," I say, beginning my wrist snaps.

"Yeah . . . It sucks all right. And it was totally out of the blue. It's like one day everything was fine and then the next, my mom said she's just not 'in love' with my dad anymore. Can you imagine?"

Yes, I can imagine. Great. Now I actually feel sorry for her.

She stares down at her glove. For a split second, she frowns. "But I guess I'm getting used to it." She looks up, standing tall. The smile is back.

She's lying. You never get used to it.

Amber wrist-snaps the ball back to me.

"Nice speed," I hear someone say to my right. I turn toward the voice and spot Zachary hanging on the fence with a basketball tucked under his arm. He waves his friends Nick Solerno and Andrew Mason (aka Missy's ex) on, telling them that he'll meet up with them at the basketball court.

"You know that Amber threw the pitch, not me, right?" I glare at Zachary. Then I focus back on Amber.

Zachary ignores me, turning to Amber. "Not only are the Wildcat pitchers hot, but they throw fire."

I look past his devious grin and stare at the twisted white and blue strings of the friendship bracelet adorning his wrist. I try not to gasp. I made that bracelet for him five years ago—*Why is he still wearing it even after we broke up?* I allow my eyes to travel up his arm, past his thick neck and his lips, to his big brown eyes. Then I catch myself mid-ogle. "Talking about the guys or the girls?" I ask.

"What do you think?" Zachary smirks.

Shifting directions, I wrist-snap the ball back to Amber. It thumps against the back fence because she's too busy staring (more like gawking) at Zachary. Her eyes widen when she realizes what she's done. Looking embarrassed, she runs after it.

Why do all girls melt at the sight of him?

I glance at Zachary again.

Okay, so he's gorgeous, a star athlete, and talks a good game, but he's also a huge player. A player that ruined what was left of our relationship by winning the three-B challenge.

"Still not talking to me?" Zachary asks, his thick lips moving with each word. Why do they look so kissable?

I glare back, wishing there was a switch in my brain I could flick to turn off the way I feel when I'm around him.

"Oh, Ky, just give in." He tilts his head. "Pretty hard not to talk to me when we live so close now. You know all you need to do is say the word and I'll be right—"

"Shhh . . ." I look around frantically and lower my voice. "You know I don't want anyone knowing. . . ."

He leans forward and his sweatshirt inches up just a bit, showing off a peek of his six-pack. "Well, can I at least say that I can't wait to see my girl take the mound again?"

My heart begins to race, and I realize that I need to put an end to this now. Before I listen to my heart instead of my brain. I opt for honesty. "You're messing with my concentration," I say, watching Amber search for the ball behind her.

"I always mess with your concentration."

Understatement of the century.

Zachary looks over at Amber, who has just gotten her grip on the ball. "Hey," he says, nodding.

I push my way in front of Amber. "Whatever."

Zachary just shakes his head. "Catch ya at my guesthouse later . . ." he whispers. Then he turns around and winks (yes, winks!) at Amber.

Amber turns pink with excitement. Her face lights up like the center-field scoreboard.

Nice.

I hear the thud of the bouncing basketball grow quieter and quieter as Zachary makes his way to the court.

Really? I think. *He had to flirt with Amber?* I can't believe even *he'd* stoop that low. On the one hand, he's telling me that he should come over. On the other, he flirts with the one girl who might actually be a threat out on the diamond.

"Guess you're glad he went away," Jessica says, interrupting my thoughts. She's standing on the other side of the pitching cage, practicing her swings with Abby. A royal blue batting helmet covers her head.

"Yeah. What a loser," Abby adds, shoving her hand into her blue batting glove.

A flush of heat creeps up my back.

What my teammates really want to say is that I'm the loser for staying with him for three years. But what they don't understand is that he really is two people—the guy they see at school and the guy he is with me.

"Yeah," I reply, unconvincingly. Then I roll my eyes, pivot, and toss the ball back to Amber.

Amber retrieves the ball and moves her arms into power

position so that her left arm is at three o'clock and her right arm is at nine o'clock. Then, she launches it back to me. The ball slaps into my glove with the force of a tornado.

How is that possible? Even her half motion is harder than my full.

"What's the deal with that guy?" Amber asks dreamily. Then, as if she wasn't just mentally undressing my ex, she sets up in her power position again and begins to throw. If I thought her wrist-snaps were powerful, they're nothing compared to when she uses her legs. My palm is already red and throbbing after only a couple of throws from her.

"It's nothing." I instinctively divert my eyes. Then I look up abruptly. "So, why Beachwood?" I ask. "Did you and your mom just move here?"

She shrugs, completely unfazed. "We didn't move. I still live with her. My dad left." Amber pauses. "Wait, how did you know I lived with my mom?"

"Lucky guess." *Since I'm the only one whose mom ditches her.*

"Originally, I wanted to go here for high school. You know, because of . . ." She looks out at the outfield and points to Danielle, a junior who rode the bench last year after barely making varsity. Her tie-dyed socks match Amber's.

"You wanted to come here because of her?" I ask, shocked that Danielle would be reason enough for someone to change dinner plans let alone schools. (She and I don't exactly get along.)

"Well, Danielle goes here and she always told me great

things about the Beachwood athletic program overall." She trails off. "But my dad had different ideas and basically made me go to my old school, Upper Crest."

"Why would he do that?" I ask, thinking that if my own father ever tried to pull a stunt like that, I'd move in with Missy and have him arrested for child endangerment.

Amber beams. "Meet the daughter of the Upper Crest Teacher of the Year!" She points to herself, giggling.

"You're kidding?" I deadpan.

"Nope. Wish I was. So when they divorced, I stayed with Mom."

Of course she did. What girl lives with her dad in a guesthouse?

I guess I get caught in my personal pity party for too long because the next thing I hear is Amber asking, "So, what's your story?"

No way I'm letting the conversation go there. "Isn't it against California High School Athletic Association rules to change schools?" I ask, shifting gears. "I mean, can't you get suspended from play for switching midyear?"

She shrugs again. "Yeah, I know the rule you're talking about—how you can't change schools to play on a different team once the school year's already started. But according to the CHSAA, a hardship is a free pass." She lets out a breath. "And the divorce is considered a hardship."

"Uh, sorry about the—"

Amber cuts me off. "I'm just so happy to get away from Upper Crest. It'll be nice to be a normal student and not just someone's daughter. Seriously, my dad knew everything I was doing. Every guy I talked to. Every grade I got. Every convo I had with my coach. It was humiliating."

Hmm . . . I allow my mind to wander into sabotage territory. "What if your dad lost his job? Would you go back?"

"What?" Amber's forehead wrinkles.

"Never mind."

Amber jogs toward me. When she's a few inches away, she leans in close, as if we're suddenly BFFs. "I wouldn't say this to other people," she whispers. "But I'm also just insanely psyched about playing for Beachwood. We could turn the program around! Can you imagine? I'm always a sucker for the underdog." She beams, hugging her glove.

Is she for real? She'd rather play for us than for a team where playoffs are a shoo-in? "I didn't know Beachwood was so pathetic," I snap.

But she doesn't hear me. Or at least, she acts like she doesn't. Instead, she turns around and takes off back to her spot.

When she's settled, I fire the ball back her way with as much power as I can muster.

Amber catches the ball and immediately starts to set up for her response. No wincing, no hand wringing, no nothing. My pitch—which must have been at least fifty miles per hour—has as little effect on her as a two-year-old carelessly placing a crushed flower into her palm.

I suck in a breath and begin to pray to anyone who will

listen. *Please deny the hardship. Please be banned. Please make Amber go away.* And then, because I'm a glutton for punishment, I decide to figure out whether she has any D-I plans. "Any idea which college you want to go to?" I ask.

"I don't know yet. I'm getting some interest and stuff. . . ." She gazes up at the cloudless sky. "But honestly, I think I'd love to go to UCLA." She raises her arm and, in one fluid motion, whips the ball back to me, dragging her leg and touching her shoulder with her bent arm.

I manage to catch the ball, but the force of her throw disrupts my balance, and I take a few steps back.

"How about you?" she asks, like nothing even happened.

"Oh, you know—to be determined." No way I'm giving Amber the satisfaction of knowing we share the same dream.

I set up on the rubber, wind up, and push off, firing a fast pitch that has been known to make catchers' hair stand on end.

The ball lands squarely in her glove. "Nice," she says. "You're good." Then she takes a giant step and fires the ball right back at me. I don't even see the thing coming before it smacks into my glove. My hand throbs in pain. Without thinking, I toss my glove to the ground and shake out my hand.

"Are you okay? I'm so sorry," she says, rushing toward me.

"Yeah, I'm fine," I answer through gritted teeth. I've been nailed before, but I can't believe I let Amber get one over me like that.

Amber glances around frantically. "I'm so, so sorry. It's my fault. I should have told you that the pitchers I warm up with usually wear padded gloves," Amber says, attempting to grab my hand.

I swipe my hand back. "Thanks for the tip," I say, using my good palm to stretch out my bruised one. There's no way I'm wearing a padded glove. I'm tougher than that.

"Are you sure you don't want ice?" Amber asks.

"No, really, I'm okay," I say, glaring at her.

"Okay, but if you change your mind—"

"I won't."

"Oh, okay." Her eyes search mine, desperate for me to accept her apology. "Seriously, Kylie, I'm sorry."

"Don't be. Just get back to your side." I shove my hand into my glove. That must have been the cue Amber was waiting for because she finally jogs back to the other side, still spilling *I'm-sorrys*.

As soon as she makes it to her spot, I wind up and unleash my response.

Amber easily catches my pitch.

Is there anything this girl can't do?

This time, before she winds up, I take a few steps back into the cage to allow her ball some time to lose some fire.

Smack.

Again, my hand screams for mercy. But I don't let it show. One time was embarrassing enough.

"What other pitches do you throw?" I ask, eager to give my hand a chance to rest.

"Fastball, curve, screwball, and drop. But my best pitch is the rise," she says.

Figures.

four

After school the next day, I head to the cafeteria to fill up my water bottle before tryouts. On my way, I try to convince myself that despite what Coach Kate said about this year being a clean slate, and despite Amber's killer rise ball, my spot is still mine. But no matter how many times I tell myself Coach Kate will stay loyal, I can't get the what-ifs out of my head.

What if Coach replaces me with Amber? What if she forgets about our history? What if instead of remembering how she approached me as an eighth grader, she decides to go for a pure power pitcher? What if she heard about last season's basketball drama? What if she ignores her own code of loyalty?

I can't allow any of that to happen. Between Zachary and Mom, I've been rejected enough lately. I don't think I can handle it if Coach dumps me too.

When I finally reach the caf, I shove my hand into the side of my Under Armour bag and pull out an empty Aquafina bottle—a dig at my dad. (He'd chafe at the plastic.) If there's one thing I'm sure of, it's that there's no way I can handle trying out against Amber without some serious fluids.

I quickly fill up my bottle and look up to see Missy standing next to me.

"What are you doing here?" I ask, looking at the pile of magazines hugged tightly to her chest.

"I . . . uh . . . What are *you* doing here?" Her periwinkle eyes bug. "And, uh . . . why are you holding a plastic water bottle?" She glares at me in mock accusation. "Hasn't your dad taught you anything? I thought he banned plastic."

"Very funny. Seriously. I thought you'd left already." I think back to when Missy stopped at my locker after the final bell. I swore she said she was going home.

"I was going to leave, but . . ." She nervously scans the cafeteria like she's looking for someone.

I follow her gaze and see Hannah Montgomery roll past us on her skateboard.

"I'm working with Hannah." Missy lets out a breath. "Remember I told you? For prom. And I joined Ms. Sealer's Fashion Club. You know, to gain some marketing experience for college. Not only do I get to add an extracurricular to my resume, but I get a cut of Hannah's profits if she ever makes it big. Smart, huh?"

I give her a look like: *Really? That Hannah?*

She whispers, "I know what you're thinking, but who better to promote than the winner of the Spring Fashion Show?"

"Are you really that desperate for extracurriculars?"

Hannah rolls her skateboard between us, stopping in front

of Missy. "Ready Freddy?" She unwraps a Hershey's Kiss and pops it in her mouth.

"Yeah . . . I'll be there in just a bit," Missy says, twisting a strand of platinum blonde hair with the index finger of her unused hand. Turning to me, she silently pleads for me to be nice to her newest meal ticket.

"What's up, Han?" I ask. "Didn't know our caf was a skate park."

"It's all about the inspiration, Ky. Chocolate and pushing my limits on the board gets me going." She rolls the skateboard with one foot.

"Oh . . ." I take a swig from my water bottle to stop myself from laughing.

"I'll meet you in Ms. Sealer's room in five," Hannah says to Missy. Then she rolls out of the cafeteria.

The second Hannah's out of sight, I let loose with my frustration. "Really, Miss?" I ask.

Missy just shrugs.

"How can you stand it?" I shove the bottle back into my bag.

"Um . . . hello? She won the Spring Fashion Show."

"Yeah, so?"

"So—and I couldn't say this to you before because she was around—but I'm just looking for someone to kind of do the work for me, you know?" She smacks her gum.

"Uh-huh."

"And anyway, I just put in my headphones when she

starts her skater babble." Missy shrugs, motioning to her ears.

"Okay, fair enough." I raise my eyebrows and throw my bag over my shoulder. "Just as long as you don't start wearing metal bottle caps around your neck as 'jewelry,' we're good."

Hannah rolls back into the cafeteria, popping the front end of her board and launching into a perfect ollie. It's so strange to see someone skateboarding in the cafeteria, I can't help but stare.

"Forget what I just said," I say, rolling my eyes.

Missy rests the magazines on a table. "I thought you were going to try to take it down a few notches. Hm?"

"When I'm around my friends, sure. But, you can't expect me to be good around *Taylor's* BFF."

"You? G—"

I cut Missy off. "Sorry, Miss. I gotta go. It's time for tryouts."

I start to make my way to the exit when I hear Missy call out, "Wait."

"Yeah?" I ask, stopping mid-stride.

"What are you going to do about prom?"

"Huh? What are you talking about?"

"I'm *talking* about revenge. We gotta make Andrew and Zach regret humiliating us last season."

I glance at the white-and-blue Beachwood clock. "How about we hash this out after you're done with your new BFF? I'll meet you at your car after practice."

"Ugh. Fine. But, seriously, where are my friends when I need them?" She makes a big show of looking around.

I chuckle. "They're at softball tryouts—where I should be. But don't worry, I'll tell them you said hi."

Before Missy can pull me deeper into her vortex, I jog out of the cafeteria, excited to take the mound again.

There's no way I'll lose Missy, my mom, Zachary, *and* softball all in the same year. The world isn't that cruel.

five

"Bring it together, girls," Coach Kate calls from the pitcher's mound after we've all had a chance to warm up with our freshmen partners.

Glad to be given a reprieve from Amber duty, I sprint over, quickly finding a spot between Jessica and Nyla. My appearance interrupts a heated discussion about the differences between the SAT and the ACT.

The sun is warm against the back of my heather-gray Beachwood Academy Softball tee, and I'm feeling surprisingly good about my prospects. Knowing that Coach likes a neat appearance, I tuck my tee into my mesh shorts. As I'm about to reach up to adjust my lucky blue-and-white hair ribbons, I feel a tug on my ponytail.

I turn around to see Chloe attempting to maneuver between me and Jessica. "Are these from last year?" she asks, touching my hair.

Doesn't she get it? Once anyone's tongue enters the vicinity of Zachary's mouth, we're no longer friends. EVER.

"Yeah, Ky. I love the ribbons," Phoenix adds.

"Thanks, Phoenix."

"Ky, how's the rise?" Emily asks as she joins us.

"It's working . . ." I answer, hoping the panic that I feel doesn't reach my face.

"What's up, Nyla?" I ask, turning toward Nyla instead. "Spending all that time in the pitching cage, I'm missing out on my Ny-and-Ky time."

Nyla laughs. "Yeah. Miss ya too."

"Speaking of the pitching cage, how's Amber?" Jessica asks.

"Does she live up to the hype?" Zoe chimes in, having just finished with her partner.

Let's talk about something else. Anything, I mentally plead. But no one hears my silent cries.

Abby, who I didn't even realize was standing there, gets nervous. "Ky? You okay?"

I force myself back to reality. And to Jessica's question about Amber. "That's your call," I say, motioning toward the field like I'm totally in control.

My friends follow my lead, turning to stare at the gaggle of girls. Some nervously tug on their glove strings. Others stare at the grass. And still others dig at the dirt with their feet. Amber is busy chatting with Danielle.

"I already have my own opinion about Amber."

"Sounds juicy," Jessica says.

"Oh, it is," I reply. Then I realize Coach Kate is about to begin her speech.

"Just a reminder that teams will be posted on Wednesday,"

she says, flanked by the assistant coaches. "Also, please make sure you have the number we gave out earlier today safety pinned to the back of your T-shirts so we know who you are. For the returning players, this is not necessary since all of you remembered to wear your practice jerseys." She scans the crowd, looking pleased.

I hope that doesn't mean I'm not doing enough to distinguish myself. Quickly, I do my own survey, mentally counting the number of teammates who aren't tucked. I breathe a sigh of relief. Only three of us remembered.

"Plus, I know who you are already." Coach grins, locking eyes with me for a split second.

My stomach doesn't just somersault, it does a round-off back handspring. I look down at my white-and-blue number seven practice jersey. After feeling anxious (to say the least) about Amber, I'm momentarily filled with a sense of ease. Amber's going to have to do a lot more than pitch to prove she's ready for varsity softball at Beachwood.

Coach continues, "Today is our first official day of tryouts. To understand what we do here at Beachwood, pay attention to the upperclassmen, as we have specific routines when we arrive at the softball field. . . ."

I take Coach's endless droning as an opportunity to sneak another peek at Amber. I guess warm-up procedures really float her boat because she's staring at Coach like she's two-time Olympic medalist Jessica Mendoza.

I tug at my glove and remind myself of what Coach

always says: "Talent alone doesn't win championships." But if it did . . . Amber's not the only one with that particular skill set. I've got it too. Enough talent to start as a freshman and sophomore. And certainly enough talent to crush Amber.

Having calmed myself with Coach's words, I force myself to pay attention.

"I would like to turn everyone's attention to the outfield fence. Does anyone notice anything worth mentioning?" She points to the fence, and I can't help but stare at the state-of-the-art scoreboard that sits at the center. The words WELCOME BACK, BEACHWOOD ACADEMY SOFTBALL scroll in red on the bottom.

The group is silent.

Then Nyla pipes up. "I do."

"Yeah, me too . . ." Emily announces.

"Yes, Nyla?" Coach Kate's lips form a straight line.

"The fence is empty."

"Exactly. The fence is empty. We have no championship or tournament banners." Coach Kate folds her arms across her chest. "But Wildcats, we're going to change that this year. We're going to change that by pushing ourselves like we never have before and by making sure that we have the absolute best talent out here on the softball diamond."

I swear for a moment Coach Kate glances at Amber. Fire burns in my stomach and I rub my palms against the sides of my matching mesh royal-blue team shorts.

I'm not giving up my position that easily.

"Remember our goal is a winning season—from day one," she continues. "By the end of the school year, we *will* have a banner hanging from that fence. And I want to reiterate: no one is safe. We're putting the best team out there regardless of who you are. So fight hard to win your spot!" Coach shouts.

The crowd responds with paralyzed silence.

Coach waits for the nervous looks to peter out. "Today, the assistants and I are going to evaluate you on your fielding. So, infielders, please go with Coach Zimmer. And outfielders, you're with Coach Dominico. Catchers, please grab your gear and follow Coach Jackie. Pitchers, you're with me," Coach says, pointing to the various assigned areas. "Now, let's get started!" Coach charges toward the pitcher's mound.

We all immediately stand up, eager to begin the tryouts. Amber somehow manages to come out of nowhere to stand next to me. Her freckled face flushes and she grins. I attempt to grin back, but I suspect I look like I'm in pain. She turns to say something to Danielle, and, overwhelmed by curiosity, I ignore my own friends and peek behind her to see what number she has pinned to her shirt.

Instantly, I regret the decision. There, taunting me, is a big number one.

"This is *so* not good," Jessica says, drumming her long concert pianist fingers against her cheek.

"We have nothing to worry about," I chime in, attempting to convince the others as much as myself.

"Yeah, it's not like this is brand new to us," Nyla adds, pushing up her Gator hoodie sleeves. "We've been here before."

"Of course *you two* aren't worried." Emily rolls her eyes. "Nyla, you're like the best player in Beachwood history. And Kylie, have you ever not played varsity?"

"Seriously," Phoenix adds, twirling a skinny braid.

"Will you guys relax? Coach is talking about the new girls," I say, taking deep breaths as I watch Amber jog toward the mound. I feel the anxiety beginning to overwhelm me and immediately shake myself out of my stupor. "Come on, girls, let's go!"

Zoe, who has been silent this whole time, looks up at me, and I give her arm a squeeze. Then she and Abby—who is also visibly quivering at this point—run out to their spots on the field. The rest of us give each other a final nod and all follow suit. Jessica, Nyla, and Phoenix join the infielders on the dirt between second and first. Chloe jogs toward right field. And Emily joins the catchers to my left.

That just leaves those of us on the mound: me, three freshmen, last year's JV pitcher, Sophia, and Amber. Clearly, there's only one real threat.

Too nervous to chat, the six of us turn to face our evaluator. I allow myself to revel in my good fortune—Coach Kate is the one scoring us. She knows me. She's the same person who just asked me to join her at the coaching clinic. She can't bench me now.

I hope.

"Okay, Wildcats. I hope you're all warmed up and ready to give us your best," Coach Kate says, holding her clipboard like a lunch tray. A radar gun balances on top. "Today, you're going to pitch off the mound without a batter. Emily, our returning catcher from last year, will catch you. I will stand behind the backstop fence and clock your speed with this." She holds up the black radar gun. "Kylie, why don't you take the mound first since you know the drill?"

The five other girls trying out for pitcher look up at me in awe. *Including Amber.* For a second, I feel like everything is normal—Coach Kate is still loyal to me. And I'm standing on the softball mound, my home away from home.

Coach tosses me the ball, and I dig my foot into the familiar soft orange dirt. Lifting her face mask, Emily winks at me from behind home plate. She knows I got this. Then she adjusts her chest protector and knee guards and crouches down.

Coach Kate, satisfied that Emily is ready to go, looks at the other girls. "The rest of the pitchers, please wait for your turns in the dugout." Turning to me, she says, "Since you should be warmed up, Kylie, why don't you throw three practice pitches and then we'll get started?" She begins flipping through the papers attached to her clipboard.

Emily gives me a nod and I take a deep breath. Then I step onto the rubber, focus, wind up, take a giant step, and push off, whipping the ball toward Emily's glove.

Smack.

"Nice work, Ky!" Emily's muffled voice shouts from behind the catcher's mask.

Nick and Andrew walk by the far fence on their way to shoot some hoops. "Killer Kylie!" they yell out. "Ow! Ow!"

Take that, Amber.

After two more perfect practice pitches, Coach Kate shouts, "Okay, let's get started." She points the radar gun at me.

Emily gives me the sign and calls out, "Fastball, outside."

Don't overthink, just throw. Coach Malone's words fill my head. I remind myself that I've done this a bazillion times before. Then I take a deep breath, wind up, push off the rubber, and fire.

"Strike!" Coach yells. "Nice pitch, Kylie." She looks down at the radar gun. "Fifty-nine."

My heart stops. *Oh my God. That's nearly what I want to top out at UCLA. I might actually be able to do this.*

I fire two more fifty-nine-mile-per-hour fastballs.

Beat that, Amber.

Emily gives me the sign for the screwball. My best pitch. I feel for the seams, wind up, twist my wrist, and fire my favorite pitch. It cuts right.

"Beautiful," Coach yells, and scribbles something on her clipboard. "Fifty-eight."

As I throw a drop and changeup, I look over at the dugout. Amber just sits there, smiling as she hugs her glove. *Enjoy the bench*, I silently tell her.

"Can I see your rise?" Coach asks, holding her pen over the last box on the evaluation sheet.

"Yeah. I mean, yes," I say, mustering up as much confidence as I can. Again my pitching coach's words echo in my ears: *Don't aim, throw.*

I dig my foot in and take a deep breath, attempting to control the butterflies at war in my stomach. I find the seams with two fingers, wind up, take a giant leap, and twist the doorknob just like I've been practicing with my spinner. The laces snap across the tips of my fingers. The ball flies from my hand, darting upward. But instead of cutting right before the plate, it rises early and way too high.

Emily reaches up to grab it. It's good, but it's far from great.

"Fifty-three. Nice work, Ky," Coach says, looking up from her clipboard. "Sophia, you're up next."

Sophia hops off the bench and tucks her glove under her

arm. She leans down, pulls up her socks, and jogs toward the mound, passing me on the way. *Let's see what you've got*, my eyes tell her.

When I enter the dugout, Amber jumps down from the bench and holds out her hand for a teammate slap.

I don't think so.

Pretending I don't see her hand, I pass her and dig into my bag for my water bottle.

"Nice work, Ky! I just knew you were going to do amazing. Do you need a water bottle?"

"Thanks, I'm good," I reply, pulling the bottle out of my bag. After yesterday's practice, I knew Amber would only be all too eager to take care of everything. And I couldn't allow that.

Taking a few more steps away from Amber, I scan for a spot in the dugout, knowing that there's no way I'm taking a seat on that bench. God forbid Coach see me there and think that I want to stay.

Ultimately, I decide to stand to the side and watch Sophia in action. Fortunately, there isn't much to watch. After five okay pitches in the high forties, Coach announces that she's seen enough. Then she calls for Amber.

"Yay!" Amber jumps off the bench and excitedly makes her way to *my* mound.

Once there, she moves her foot around, manicuring the dirt with her head down. I do my best not to jump up and strangle her right in front of everyone. Nothing irritates me more than when the visiting pitcher digs into *my* mound. And now Amber has the gall to do it. Ruin *my* smooth surface.

I take another swig from my water bottle.

"Are you ready?" Coach asks Amber, a whopping five practice pitches later.

"Yup." Amber beams. "Ready as I'll ever be."

I roll my eyes, wishing that Missy were here to crack jokes and cut the tension.

Emily calls the pitch. "Fastball inside."

Amber winds up.

Smack. The ball explodes into Emily's glove. The power of Amber's pitch pushes Emily back a bit. Just like it did me yesterday.

This is not good.

I contemplate sticking my fingers in my ears so I don't have to hear the radar gun reading.

"Strike," Coach calls out. "Nice pitch, Amber." She looks down at the radar gun. "Sixty-two."

Sixty-two? Are you kidding me? No, that's not possible. Coach is probably just trying to make Amber feel comfortable by rounding up.

Emily tosses the ball back to Amber. Then, giving Amber the sign, she calls out, "Screwball!"

I chuckle to myself. The screwball is *my* pitch. There's no way she's better than me at the screwball.

Amber sets up, stares at Emily's glove, and nods at the sign. She winds up, takes a giant step, and fires.

Smack.

"Strike," Coach announces. "Fifty-seven."

I breathe a sigh of relief. Amber can't touch my screwball. I threw it faster. I threw it sharper. I've got it in the bag.

Amber pitches three more in the high fifties before Coach shouts, "Okay, Amber, I think we've seen enough. Nice job." She looks over at the dugout. "Lauren, you're up."

A freshman brunette with two braids hops off the bench.

"Wait!" Amber shouts. "I have one more pitch to show you."

"Amber, I've seen plenty. Nice job."

"Please . . . I haven't had the opportunity to show you my best pitch." Amber leans forward, clinging to her glove.

Keep crying, Amber. Coach hates whiners.

Coach pulls the pen from behind her ear, checks her Nike watch, and scribbles something on her clipboard. "I guess we have time for one more pitch. Go ahead."

"Rise," Amber announces, suddenly confident.

Amber drags more dirt on the mound, and I have to stop myself from yelling out, *She's acting like she has more poise than Jennie Finch, but have you seen all her nervous habits?* Then she lets out a deep breath, winds up, and fires, pushing all her power toward Emily.

Thud.

We all watch in amazement as Amber's blurry pitch cuts up at the last second.

Coach looks down at her radar gun and her eyes pop. She shakes it and looks again, more closely. Finally, she says in astonishment, "Sixty-six."

A perfect rise ball.

seven

Still bitter about Amber's rise ball, I take off for the student parking lot the second tryouts are over. Luckily, one thing does go my way—Missy's car is still sitting there. At least she stuck around long enough to drive me home. I breathe a sigh of relief that I don't have to call my dad.

"Thank God this day is over," I announce as I slide into the passenger seat of her black BMW three series, a birthday gift from Daddy. "And thanks so much for waiting."

Missy looks up from the magazine she was reading. "No prob," she says. "Everything okay?"

"I don't want to talk about it . . ." I say, tossing my bag onto her backseat.

"You sure?" she asks, doing the same with her magazine before putting the car into reverse.

"Yeah," I say, tersely. I know Missy means well, but right now I'm not in the mood for conversation. I close my eyes and remind myself that I won't have to bum rides forever. In a few months, I'll finally take my driver's test. Then hopefully I'll get a car, assuming my dad cuts loose with some cash.

I lean back into the bucket seat, letting the plush tan leather envelop me. As we pull out of the school parking lot, Missy waves to Brooke Lauder in her Benz. Brooke seems pleased to see us, but I don't have the patience for her right now. The last thing I need to hear is "tales of the life of a tortured model." I glance her way for a split second and then turn on my phone, checking to see if there are any e-mails with a *ucla.edu* address in my inbox. (Not that there are likely to be. Especially after today's performance.)

"Okay then . . ." Missy looks at me out of the corner of her eye.

We sit in silence, driving past the huge, stone Beachwood sign and through the campus's iron gates. Once we reach my neighborhood, crazy thoughts begin to swirl in my brain.

Oh my God. I'm screwed.

Oh my God. I'm going to lose my spot.

Oh my God. I'm going to lose softball.

Oh my God. I have no future.

Oh my God. Oh my God. Oh my God.

"Ky, you all right over there?" Missy asks. Clearly, my insanity has become palpable.

I rest my head against the headrest. "Uh-huh."

Missy isn't buying it. "What's that?" she asks, glancing at my phone.

"College stuff," I say, holding up my phone for her to see. "Or, should I say, what I wish was college stuff."

"Seriously, Ky. I don't know what you're worried about.

You've got it in the bag. The recruiters will be knocking down your door. And if they don't, you can always walk-on at any school you want." She looks at me encouragingly.

"What door?" I smirk. "You mean the one at the guest-house that doesn't even belong to us?"

"I assume you still have a door," she replies.

I stare blankly back.

"You know. That thing you enter. It swings back and forth. There's usually a knob."

A hint of a smile creeps its way onto my face.

Missy takes this to mean that all is better. "Whose guest-house are you staying at, anyway?" she asks, totally unaware that the guesthouse in question belongs to the family of a certain ex-boyfriend of mine.

I quickly run through my mental files to remember which lie I told her. "Remember? My dad's friend—our neighbor's."

She pulls in front of the FOR SALE sign at my former beach house, peering into the adjacent yards. She then drives five blocks in the wrong direction, eventually arriving at someone else's guesthouse. The one I've been lying about living in. "I hate to say this because I know you're going to take it the wrong way . . ." she says.

I look at her like, *Are you kidding me? You lead with that?*

Missy ignores my response. "But I still don't get it. Why would your dad move before the house sold?"

I shrug my shoulders. "No clue." I leave out the fact that

my dad isn't exactly interested in having his living arrangements funded by my mom.

"So once your house sells, where are you going?"

"I don't know. . . ." I grab my bag, hoping that my neighbors don't notice I've been spending an exorbitant amount of time parked in front of their house.

"Wait, Ky!" she calls out. (A little too loudly if you ask me, considering that I haven't even exited the car yet.) "When are you going to take your driver's test?"

"Huh?"

"You know the test we all took last year?"

"Oh yeah . . . that." The divorce had me so shaken over the summer that I skipped out on the lessons my mom scheduled for me, which meant that the test was then kind of out of the question.

"Maybe picking out brand-new wheels will make you feel better."

"Doubtful . . ."

"Well, maybe this will help pep you up. I still haven't told you about my revenge plan! For the boys." She raises one eyebrow.

As much as I don't have room for this in my life right now, I can't help but be intrigued. "What kind of plan?" I ask.

"Just a little list of our own."

"Sounds fascinating," I reply, egging her on. "Count me in." I shut the car door behind me.

Missy rolls down the window. "Oh, I will." She winks.

I begin walking up the stone driveway of our neighbor's house praying for Missy to leave, when I hear her call out, "Wait just one sec, Ky."

I turn around.

"You dodged me on the guesthouse question. Tell me, is the Collins family impoverished? It's okay. Even Donald Trump filed for bankruptcy."

"Keep studying those SAT words," I say. "Don't worry about the Collins family. We're just fine. Thanks for the ride."

Missy grins, looking satisfied. Then she waves and pulls away.

I hate lying to Missy. But I can't risk telling her the truth. It's embarrassing enough to live in someone's guesthouse. But it's way more embarrassing when that guesthouse belongs to Zachary's parents.

When Missy's taillights disappear around the corner, I scale down my neighbor's driveway, saying a silent prayer of thanks that no one's come out to arrest me for trespassing. Then I trek the five blocks inland toward the Murphys' mini-estate.

Once I reach the Murphys' main house, a six-bedroom yellow stucco behemoth, I walk up the steep stone driveway, passing my dad's navy Prius along the way. Then I push through the white fence into the backyard. I glance at their half-size basketball court and traipse along the path through their immaculate garden, resisting the urge to step on their flowers and plants. Taking a not-entirely-necessary jaunt across their white-lit gazebo, I finally arrive at what I like to call our cottage—a two-bedroom stucco guesthouse. Currently, it plays home to two of three Collinses. Previously, it served as *casa de* Zachary and Zoe's nanny. Either way, it's kind of a poor excuse for a primary residence.

I dig into my bag for the equally tiny key. And then, giving up on any pretense of sanity, I peek behind me. Zachary's second-story window glows brightly. Like a homing beacon tempting me 24/7.

He's home. *Great.*

I force myself to look away and resume opening the front door of the guesthouse. Immediately my senses are assaulted by the potent smell of honeysuckle soy aromatherapy candles. A wave of heat hits my face.

"Shut the door." My dad speed-walks toward me, holding a glass of thick green liquid. His bare feet and choice of clothes—charcoal biker shorts—tell me what I'm in store for. "Don't let the heat out," he says.

Our furniture—tiny beige matching tuxedo chairs and an abaca ottoman—is pushed up against the sidewall to make room for at least a dozen multicolored yoga mats. Scantily clad ladies bend over in painful-looking triangle poses, the sweat beads on their bodies threatening to spill over onto our living room floor.

"Please slip in quickly on Mondays, Wednesdays, and Fridays," my dad whispers as he hurries past me. He wipes away beads of sweat of his own from his freshly shaved head.

That was something he adopted after his mini–heart attack a year ago—shaving his head to cover his balding. The other was a midlife-crisis-style career change.

Exactly one year ago this May, my dad quit his real job and jetted off to India to study yoga. Two months later, when he returned, he slowly began his transformation toward his new career goal—to become Southern California's premier yoga instructor. A month after that, my type A mom couldn't take his babble anymore. (As she eventually told me, she worked really hard, and he was doing *what*?) So, she filed for divorce, and left.

And honestly, I don't blame her. For years, my parents would fight in private when they thought I couldn't hear them. And all of their fights were about the same thing—how my mom actually wanted practical things and my dad didn't.

I glance back at my dad and think about what other families must be doing right now—finishing dinner, watching television. And here we are at yoga night. So, yeah, I guess I do blame my mom for one thing: leaving me with *him*.

Wanting to escape my dad as quickly as possible, I take a quick right down the narrow hallway to my bedroom. I sigh in disgust when it takes me all of ten seconds to arrive at my door—I still can't believe my dad voluntarily downgraded from fifteen rooms to five just so he didn't have to depend on my mom to pay the mortgage. On the plus side, my Lab Kibbles is waiting there to greet me. She stands up on her hind legs in front of my door and slobbers all over me with warm, sloppy kisses. I giggle and squat down to pet her long golden fur.

"Hey, girl. Who's a cutie? Who do I love?" I scratch underneath her chin and she wags her tail excitedly. Then I stand up and push open the door to my room, spinning the doorknob just as I do my screwball.

From there, things take a turn for the worst. Kibbles follows me into my room, and I'm so caught up in playing with her that I don't notice the softball glove I left on the ground. Naturally, I trip over it and collapse onto my bed. In a way, I guess it's good because my bed—the only piece of furniture I was allowed to keep during the move—is there to cushion my fall. But all it does is manage to remind me of how small my room is. There's literally a whopping two feet between my door and the foot of my bed.

For a moment, I just lie there, thinking about how once upon a time things were good—how my mom and I picked out the bed together; how Missy and I used to have sleepovers where we'd lie on this very bed and imagine what prom would be like; how Zachary and I used to lie there in each other's arms, telling each other that we'd always be there.

A single tear trickles down my face. I roll over to my side, placing my hand on the bamboo cotton duvet. The duvet feels stiff to the touch. I stifle a scream. Just another thing to make it impossible to forget that every friggin' thing in this house is biodegradable. Even what are supposedly *my* linens.

I pull myself off my bed and close my blinds, just in case

Zachary decides to indulge in his habit of knocking on my window at all hours. Then I grab my pink iPod off my bamboo night table and lie back on my bed. Shoving the white earbuds into my ears, I blast my "Chill Out" mix. "Need You Now" courses from the headphones, bringing me back to the first time I heard the song: Zachary and I were hanging out after his parent's annual Fourth of July bash. Tucked away in "our spot"—the corner of the beach where the cliffs form two perfect chairs—Zachary and I cuddled together as he jokingly serenaded me. *If there was ever a perfect moment . . .*

I glance out the window that overlooks the back of Zachary's house. He's right there. Only yards away. It would be so much easier if I could just talk to him tonight. Right now. He would be able to make sense of this Amber mess.

Instantly, everything hits me like one of Amber's fastballs. The tears flow. Within seconds, my face looks like a car skidded across my cheeks.

Dad is nuts. Mom left. Zachary is gone. And I don't even have the guts to tell Missy where I live.

Softball is all I have left. If I lose softball, I'll lose Kylie.

eight

It's Wednesday. D-day. The day Coach Kate posts the team roster. The day I find out if Amber's transfer has destroyed my life. And I'm stuck in ninth period pre-calc like someone in prison waiting for parole.

With my notebook spread out in front of me, I watch Mrs. Cunningham frantically grade papers. Then I stare at the clock over the door, tapping my pink pencil eraser to the beat of the skinny second hand as it slowly makes its way toward twelve. Then to three, to six, to nine, and back to twelve again. Ten whole minutes until the end of the school day. Ten whole minutes until I find out if I'm the starting pitcher.

"Psst . . ." Phoenix hands me a folded-up piece of lined notebook paper.

I grab it and smooth it open, laying it flat on my notebook.

Good luck! xoxo Phoenix

Good luck? Why should I need good luck? Great. Even Phoenix has lost faith in me.

"Thanks," I whisper in reply, breathing in and out to

remind myself that she only has my best intentions at heart. Then I look over at Missy's empty seat. Of all days for Missy to be out with a cold, today is the absolute worst. As much as I've been trying to tell myself that everything is going to be okay, the fact is that after three days of tryouts, Amber and I are neck and neck. Or at least what I'd like to think of as neck and neck—her pitches averaged around sixty-two miles per hour, topping out at sixty-six. Mine were around fifty-eight, topping out at sixty. And then there's her rise ball . . .

But, as I keep reminding myself, regardless of how hard she throws, I'm the one with the Beachwood experience. I'm the one Coach Kate should go with.

My thoughts are interrupted by the sounds of Hannah ripping up a magazine to my left. (Yes, she's a freshman in pre-calculus. In addition to being a design prodigy, she's a math superstar.) In front of me, Missy's ex, Andrew Mason, leans back in his chair, audibly bragging to his friends, Brett Davidson and Nick Solerno, about last season's basketball record.

"It's hard being this good," Andrew announces, folding his hands behind his head.

"I know what you mean. Second in the state is hard to top," Nick adds, checking his cell.

Brett smirks, and I can't help but butt in. "Really, Nick? Getting a lot of important messages? Don't want to miss one from Mommy."

"Ha ha . . ." The other guys each start to laugh, but then, with one quick look from Nick, realize whose side they should be on.

Quickly, he attempts to regain control of the conversation. "So, Kylie, how's the 'softy ball' team shaping up this year?" He turns around to face me, snickering. "Word is the program might get cut if you guys don't shape up. . . ."

Andrew and Brett chuckle behind him.

"Shut up, Nick," Phoenix pipes up, eager to come to my aid.

I hold up my hand, telling her to stop. There's no way I'm letting that one slide. "Whatever," I say, rolling my eyes. "Is that all you've got?"

Nick elbows Brett, urging him to do his part. But Brett doesn't budge. Instead, he shifts in his chair, looking visibly uncomfortable.

Nick takes this as an opportunity to continue. "Not even close, Ky. How hard is it to hit a giant yellow ball?" he jabs.

I meet him insult for insult. "Well, clearly, it's too hard for *you*. Don't you remember PE last year?" I ask, letting out a sigh. Then I look down at my paper and pretend to work on the assignment.

Nick is silent.

I look back up. "Oh, do you need to go to the nurse because you're having trouble remembering things? Let me remind you: I struck you out."

"She's got you there," Andrew says, now glancing at *his*

phone out of the corner of his eye. (I'd bet anything that Missy texted him despite all that revenge garbage.)

"Yeah, Nick, I saw her sit you down with three pitches," Brett adds, jabbing Nick in the arm.

Nick turns to Brett. "Now you decide to talk!" Then he shrugs. "I was having an off day."

"Then every day must be an off day," I say, pretending to yawn.

Suddenly, the bell rings. I jump out of my seat, grabbing my belongings. "Catch ya later, boys!" I call out, preparing to run out the door. Then, turning around, I decide to leave Nick with one final thought. "Good luck with that hand-eye coordination. If you need any help, I know of a great Little League team you can sign up for. Not sure if they're looking for people who can't hit the ball, though . . ."

Before any of them can respond, I turn around and tear out of pre-calc, smiling as I hear Andrew and Brett laughing uncontrollably behind me. Then I sprint toward the locker room. A crowd surrounds the bulletin board, but I don't let that stop me. I push through to the front and scan the list.

I drag my finger down the names, searching for mine, and there it is in black and white at the bottom.

Amber McDonald—starting pitcher
Kylie Collins—alternate

My life is officially over.

nine

I stand openmouthed for a few seconds, attempting to get over the initial shock. Tears begin to trickle down my cheeks despite my attempts to keep them at bay.

"Ky?" I hear someone say behind me.

"Is she okay?" someone else whispers.

"I don't think she's starting this year . . ." another person guesses.

The murmurs only add insult to injury. I quickly wipe away the tears to avoid any further embarrassment. Ignoring the other girls, I charge down the hall and right into Coach's office.

The door slams behind me. "Coach, how could you do this to me? You've known me since I was in eighth grade. I've been your starting varsity pitcher for the last two years," I plead, the desperation reaching my face as I cross my arms in front of my chest.

Coach Kate looks up from her desk and motions for the assistant coaches, who are currently seated on the other side of her desk, to leave. They take one look at me and scurry away, like ants. Coach reaches for her mug. "I know I'm all about keeping the doors of communication open, Kylie, but next time you slam my door, you'll cause the team laps."

"Sorry," I mumble.

She takes a slurping sip of her Starbucks.

"Look, you know how much this season means to me." I fall into one of the now unused fabric chairs in front of her desk. "No D-I scout will ever look at a benchwarmer."

Coach glances at the clock above the door. "I knew you would have this type of reaction, Kylie. But, I also want to remind you that this year is very important to Beachwood Softball."

"I know, you told us: tournaments, championships, banners." I pause. "And *your* job." I stare at her.

Coach raises her eyebrows. "I know this is hard. And I appreciate all that you have done for B-Dub Softball, but it's time the program moves in another direction."

I watch Coach's lips continue to move, but I'm so shocked, I can't even make out what's spewing from her mouth. I must be dreaming. No one suffers this much bad luck in six short months.

I shake my head, focusing my attention just in time to hear Coach Kate say, "Amber has what it takes to take our program to new heights. She's what we need to ensure that Beachwood Softball has a real future."

This can't be happening. This has to be some sort of joke. Like that reality show that punks people. I look around for someone hiding behind the corner plant with a video camera.

"But . . ." I begin.

"No buts, Kylie. I had no choice but to go with Amber. I realize this is difficult for you, and I'm truly sorry to pull the rug out from under you like this. But you've seen Amber's velocity. And you know as well as I do that her rise ball is unbeatable. It's terrible that you got caught in the crosshairs, but if you think about the team, you'll agree that she has what it takes to lead us to the Desert Invitational and quite possibly to a championship." Coach clears her throat.

My breath is shallow. My hands are shaking. I grasp at straws. "But . . . I can win us a banner with my screwball and my leadership and my knowledge of Beachwood Softball and . . ."

Coach Kate lets out a deep breath and says the only thing that could make this worse. "I'm sorry, Kylie, but I really don't think you can."

ten

I rush out of Coach Kate's office—there's no way I'm crying in front of the coaching staff still lingering in the hallway. It's bad enough they think I'm not good enough to start. I'm not going to let them see my pain too.

I look around frantically for Missy, and then it hits me: she's not here. No one is. And even if she were, she's so obsessed with Hannah Montgomery and beefing up her college app that she might not even notice me.

My life is over. My softball buds are going to toss me out like yesterday's lunch. No more Killer Kylie. No more Captain Kylie. No more anything. Amber will snatch up my spot as team leader just like she snatched up my spot on the mound.

When I turn the corner, I run smack into Martie, Beachwood's newest athletic director and resident soccer coach. Martie knows me from this past basketball season—she stepped in to serve as assistant coach after one of our regular coaches had to take a leave of absence.

"Kylie, are you okay?" Martie asks, lowering the folder she was carrying.

"Hey, Coach," I say, diverting my eyes and feeling too keyed up to stand still, let alone chat. As much as everyone in our school loves Martie, she's seen me at my worst—I wasn't exactly a sweetheart during basketball season—so I sincerely doubt that she's on my side.

"Kylie, I really think we should talk," Martie continues.

"No, really, that's okay." I attempt to walk around Martie, but she blocks my way. She has that look in her eye. I've seen it before—when Taylor was struggling last season. Here it comes . . . Martie's magic touch. Martie is known to show up and talk athletes off the ledge.

"Look, I heard about the roster. And I know how hard you've worked." Martie brings the folder up to her chest.

I swallow a lump. Feeling a tear about to roll down my cheek, I pretend to erase mascara from under my eyes. Mom always said it's better to be a princess than a cry baby.

"Do you still love softball?" Martie asks. Her deep brown eyes stare intently into mine.

"Of course I do," I say, scanning the hallway for any signs of my teammates. If Emily or Phoenix spot me talking to Martie, they'll pretend to take pity on me. And I just can't have that.

Martie ignores my frantic glances. "Then that's all that matters," she says, smiling. "All that matters is you love the game. Playing time, teammates, college, you can't control any of that. All you can control is your attitude, your training, and your respect for the game."

I roll my eyes. If Martie was any preachier, we'd have to get her a pulpit.

She continues, "Maybe you should try out another position. I heard you're quite a force at second for your ASA team. You should petition Coach Kate to let you work out there."

Yes, I do work out at second with my ASA team. But it's not as exciting as the mound. I'm a pitcher. Period. If I'm forced to warm the bench in college, that's one thing. Then I'll think about turning myself into a utility player. But not this year. Not my junior season. No Division I school is going to recruit a pitcher who can't even start on her high school team. And anyway, what does Martie know about softball? Nothing. *Stick to soccer, Martie.*

"No offense, Martie." I straighten out my shoulders and swallow the tears. "Just because you decided to settle for coaching a bunch of high school kids after your dreams were shattered doesn't mean the rest of us should just give up."

Martie's face falls. She clears her throat.

Before she can say anything else, I adjust my Beachwood bag on my shoulder and stomp down the hallway.

So much for the attitude redo.

eleven

Amazingly, one thing does work out for me today: the locker room is deserted, so there's no one there to see me bawl my eyes out.

I find a spot on the oak bench in the back corner and hug my legs to my chest, burying my head in my knees. Immediately, the tears start pouring out in steady streams. That is, until I hear the door click close.

"Hey."

Startled, I glance up and am met with Zachary's big chocolate eyes. His single dimple pops as he gingerly wipes a tear from my cheek with one finger. A basketball is tucked under his arm.

"How did you get in here?" I ask, using the back of my hands to dab my eyes.

He wrinkles his forehead in concern. "Ky, you're my girl. I made it my job to check out the roster. And then I saw you run in here. Are you okay?"

"Of course I'm *not* okay!" I yell. And then, realizing that I just gave the dirtball more ammunition, I quickly pull away.

Zachary takes this as a sign that I need his advice. He gently drops the basketball and sidles up on the bench next to me. "Kylie, you'll get through this. You always come out on top."

For a second, I almost let myself fall into Zachary's arms. It feels so good to hear him say that to me. Especially after all this time . . . But then, I catch myself and retreat further in the opposite direction.

Unfortunately, this isn't enough to stop him. "Remember when you were ten and you didn't make the club soccer team?" he asks, reaching out to rub my shoulders from a distance.

I attempt to resist. But then, I can't help it—chills run down my spine. "What does that—"

He continues massaging me. "Everything. Instead of letting it get you down, you tried out for field hockey. And then you know the rest . . ."

"Yeah, I learned that hockey sticks are much more annoying to carry around than you'd think."

"Ha ha, well, that"—Zach laughs—"and you found out you were a way better field hockey player than you ever were a soccer player."

I swivel around to face him. "What? Are telling me to try out for another sport? First, Martie wants me to give up pitching and now you want me to switch sports?" I cross my arms in front of my chest.

"No. Not at all. I'm just—"

I interrupt him. "And anyway, I was ten and that stuff wasn't as important."

"Well, what about when you were eight and you were so sick and tired of the tiaras and pageants? You thought it was pretty important to tell your mom you didn't want to do the whole pageant circuit anymore."

I pick the basketball up off the floor and begin bouncing it ever so slightly against the bench. "What does that even have to do with softball?"

"Remember, your mom accused you of quitting because she said you were frustrated that you couldn't win?"

Now I know where he's going with this. I hang my head.

Tenderly, he grabs the bouncing basketball from me and places it back on the ground. Then he cups my chin, gently lifting it with his hand so I'm forced to stare at him. "But you decided to prove your mom wrong, didn't you? To show her that even though you hated pageants, you could still win. And so you did. A few times." He grins. "I still remember the look on your mom's face the first time they crowned you."

I don't know if it's because of how much I want another crown—the one worn by the prom princess—or the mention of my mom, but the flood of tears fills my eyes once again.

"Once you put your mind to something, even if it's something you hate, like pageants, you can do anything, Ky. Imagine if you focused all your energies on softball what you could do. Amber wouldn't stand a chance."

At this point, I'm sobbing so hard I'm shaking. Normally, this isn't something anyone would do in front of an ex-boyfriend. But Zachary is so much more than a former flame.

He's seen me cry a zillion times before. Even more than Missy. He's my best friend. Or at least he was . . .

Zachary moves his hand from my chin and wraps his big thick arms around my shoulders to steady me as I sob.

I feel myself give in and sink into his embrace. But then I stiffen.

What am I doing? I can't do this right now.

No matter what Zachary says, he went too far last season. He just can't be trusted.

I push him away and start to hyperventilate. "Don't think you can just waltz in here and start hugging me and take advantage of me because I've had a bad day."

Zachary grins. "Who's trying to take advantage? I miss you."

I try to breathe. "You miss me? Good." I sniffle. "You're the one who messed this up."

"And I've regretted that every minute of every day since. You're the only one who gets me. Neighbor." He tilts his head to the side. "Think of all the time we're wasting being mad at each other. Who knows how long you'll be in my backyard?"

"Whatever." I roll my tired eyes. Tired from crying and tired of Zachary's ridiculous lines.

"I'm serious, Ky. I just can't take it anymore. . . ." He looks up at me, then at the clock. And then he quotes "our song": "It's a quarter after three and I'm all alone and I need you now." He grins.

Yeah, he needs me all right. Seriously? Does he think Lady Antebellum will really work on me? But he keeps singing, and before I know it, I can't stop myself from smiling back. "You're crazy . . ." I say, attempting to hide my uninvited grin. That's something else Zachary could always do. Turn my tears into giggles in minutes.

"Seriously, Ky. Do you know how many times I've wanted to knock on your window and talk to you?"

"Uh. You do . . ." I think back to the hundreds of taps I've had to ignore since we moved in.

"No, I mean, I really need you. You know I can't cope in that house without someone to talk to about it all. You're the only one that knows. . . ."

About his dad. That's what he means. I'm the only one who knows about his dad—who's a closet alcoholic.

"And there's something I've been meaning to bring up," Zachary continues.

What? Is his dad going to rehab again? Did he have a bad night? A bad week? A bad month? My stony facade melts. I allow myself to stare deeply into Zachary's eyes. When it comes to his dad, I can't keep up the charade of not caring.

That's all Zachary needs to see. He falls down on one knee and grabs my hand. Then he pops the question every girl at Beachwood wants to hear.

"Kylie, will you go to the prom with me?"

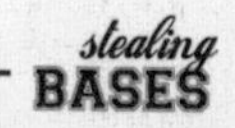

twelve

"Come on . . ." Missy pleads with me the following Saturday night. "We're going to Pinkberry. . . . You know the brownie bites are amazing." She pulls up in front of the yogurt shop.

I pick my head up from the cool glass and shrug. Missy's right—I could use a dose of chocolate right now. Maybe it will pick me up off the floor. Since I lost my starting position, it's like I'm numb. I can barely bring myself to think about prom. Or about the invite I haven't answered yet. And let me just say this: it's hard to avoid someone (aka Zachary) when you literally live right in his backyard.

"Anyway, Jess and Tamika tell me you've been sulking the whole time I was out sick. . . ." Missy flips open the visor and checks her raw nose in the reflection, dabbing it with her index finger. "Urgh. My nose will never look the same."

"I'm not sulking," I lie.

But the truth is that I totally have been. Bad. The only thing I can bring myself to do is watch last year's softball games. Over and over again. I've been trying to study the film, to attempt to see what changed, to figure out why Coach went with Amber instead of me. But I keep coming back to the same conclusion: whatever happened, it doesn't matter. I *have* to earn my spot back.

"Yeah, you're definitely sulking . . ." Missy adds.

"Whatever." I roll my eyes.

"Pouter," Missy teases.

"Princess," I joke. The nickname brings a smile to my face for a half a second—it's from Missy's Disney period. But then it hits me—princess, prom princess, my mom, Zachary's invite . . . I let out a sigh.

Missy rubs her glossed lips together. "The only person who still calls me princess is Andrew Mason, and that's exactly how he should treat me for eternity after his lame attempt at being Beachwood's biggest bad boy."

"Not exactly the bad-boy type, huh?"

"Andrew is about as bad boy as Elmo."

We burst into giggles.

"Now, stop being such a downer. Think of tonight as a Pinkberry pick-me-up."

I shrug. Without wheels of my own, it's not like I really have a say anyway. I turn to look at the store entrance and discover that it's mobbed. "I hate how *everyone* goes here," I whine.

"Uh, hello? It's not like that takes away from the tangy goodness."

I'm about to make some comment about how all that tanginess is clearly getting to Missy's head when she pulls into

a spot, and I notice the car parked next to us: Tamika's white jeep. Out come Abby, Zoe, Eva, and Jessica. Then in pulls Violet Montgomery, Hannah's ultra-popular sister, in her silver Mercedes. Sure enough, Hannah and Taylor pile out. "I thought it was just me and you tonight. . . ."

"Me, you, and the basketball team," Missy says, in between applications of pink lip gloss. "Because I don't think I can deal with your *oh-my-God, the-world-is-ending* attitude for one more second without some additional reinforcements."

"Hannah too?"

"She's getting me into college, remember?"

I stare at her blankly.

"Ky, I may be trying to rescue you from your whole woe-is-me moment, but Mama's gotta think about the future."

I shake my head in mock disbelief and step out of the car.

"Ky!" Violet calls out to me from the driver's seat of her Mercedes. She puts down her phone as I approach. "Late practice today?" Violet's nose crinkles as she scans my outfit—shorts, a practice tee, and my Adidas slides.

I look down at my choice of attire—it's painfully obvious that I have nowhere to go on a Saturday night. "Uh. Yeah."

Violet leans in through the open window. "Why don't you and Missy ditch these losers and hang out with us tonight?" She giggles, glancing at her sister. Then she places her hand over her mouth in fake shock, as if just realizing that she may not have been out of hearing range. "That is. After you change."

"Love to, Vi. But I can't ditch my girls."

"Good point. How would they know what to order without you?" Violet replies sarcastically.

"Right." I pause and my mind goes where it shouldn't. "Is Zachary going out tonight?"

Why did I let that slip out?

She narrows her eyes. "Why do you care? Thought you guys were *finito*."

"Yeah, we are. It's just"—I struggle for a response—"that I'm worried he's lost without me. You know how *boys* are. . . ."

"Oh, I *do*. And Zach is the worst of them. He's kind of like a lost little puppy."

"He is?" I ask, momentarily full of hope.

"Yeah, a lost little puppy who'd hump anything in sight!"

"Yeah . . ." I break out laughing. It's the only thing to do. "Too bad he's a stray."

"Ooh, I'm gonna tell him you said that!"

"Uh—I'm counting on it."

"Alrighty, well, gotta bounce. Catch ya on the flip," she announces. Then she pulls away.

When I walk over to my friends, they're already waiting in line, deep in conversation.

"Tamika, did you see the sketch I sent you?" Hannah asks, looking lost without her skateboard.

Tamika's face lights up. "Yup. I opened it yesterday."

"And . . . What do you think?" Missy asks, rubbing her hands together.

Tamika breaks into a wide smile. Out of nowhere, a toddler bumps into her.

"Sorry." The harried mother follows close behind the boy.

See what I mean? Crowded.

Tamika regains her balance. "Anyway. I love it! Especially the color."

"Apricot is a great shade for you . . ." Hannah says as we reach the counter.

I look up to read the menu and find that I'm face-to-face with Dwight, Tamika's ex. I always forget that he works part-time at Pinkberry.

"Looks like apricot is a good color for you too, Dwight," I say, motioning to his official Pinkberry collared shirt. In addition to being Tamika's ex, Dwight is one of Zachary's teammates and yet another three-B offender. So, he's definitely deserving of my full-on wrath.

Dwight adjusts his beige apron in an attempt to hide his shirt from view. It doesn't work.

"Nice apron." I smirk.

"Oh, you know I make this look good," Dwight replies, all macho man.

I laugh. "Uh-huh. If that's what you tell yourself . . ."

Oblivious, Hannah interrupts. "Excuse me, can I order?"

Dwight turns to face her. "I'm sorry. Welcome to Pinkberry. Would you like to try one of our original flavors?"

"No, I know what I want. An original with Fruity Pebbles and chocolate chips, please," Hannah says.

Fruity Pebbles? Seriously?

I look around for Missy and notice that she's come to stand next to Hannah. "Are you adding the silk to Tamika's dress like you were talking about?" she asks, bright eyed.

I stifle a major sigh. She's way more into the whole Hannah thing than she's letting on. Marketing experience for college—*yeah, right.*

"Do I hear you talking about my girl's prom dress?" Dwight asks.

"*Your* girl?" Tamika asks. "Sorry, but I think you may have the wrong person."

Good for her, I think. The "my girl" part almost made me want to take Hannah's yogurt and throw it at him.

I'm about to give Tamika a hug so she knows I understand what she's going through when I hear Dwight say, "Oh, you'll always be my girl." And then, turning to the group, "I can't wait to see it. Tamika looks amazing no matter what she wears."

The two of them beam at each other, and I have to stop myself from gagging. *He's definitely hanging out with Zachary way too much.*

Then he turns to the rest of us. "Anything else, ladies?"

Eva and Jessica order, followed by Zoe and Abby. I follow suit, paying as quickly as possible. Then I grab my cup and—ignoring the fact that Taylor still hasn't ordered—I usher my teammates along, attempting to locate a table. As usual, it's standing room only.

"Told you guys. It's crawling with tourists." I make a big show of gesturing to the full tables, and that's when I notice Missy's sweater. "Uh, Miss . . ."

She looks down and spots a blotch of yogurt on her cashmere.

"Ew!" She digs into her bag and pulls out a tissue.

I roll my eyes and spoon a brownie into my mouth.

"Beach?" Jessica suggests, pointing her plastic spoon south toward the surf.

"Ugh . . . we'll never find parking, and it's a ten minute walk," Missy whines, desperately trying to erase the soon-to-be stain.

"Someone hasn't worked out since basketball," I say, bumping into Missy. She deserves it.

Missy hip checks me back. "Someone is an Oscar the Grouch today."

She's got me there.

Once we reach the beach, the cool ocean wind whips our napkins, sending Eva's sailing across the sand. She takes off after it, grabbing it before it soars into the surf. Taylor arrives a few seconds later.

The fog has lifted from earlier, but with the sun setting, it leaves a sharp chill in the air. I pull my Beachwood Softball warm-up jacket tight around my chest and, as I do so, my stomach sinks. *I guess this will be the last jacket I ever get with the* P *for pitcher on the sleeve.*

I'm about to share this great revelation with Missy when I realize that she's already taken a seat on the semi-deserted beach and is busy flipping through the prom issue of *Seventeen* with her new BFF, Hannah. Disgruntled, I spoon another scoop of Pinkberry into my mouth and squeeze in next to Jessica.

As Missy turns the pages, I catch sight of a prom ad from out of the corner of my eye. The photo is difficult to miss—the guy pictured looks just like Zachary, dimple and all. Immediately, my mind flips back to the unanswered invite. *What am I going to do about the prom?*

"Is that the dress you're using as inspiration?" Abby asks, looking at the ad over Hannah's shoulder. She tucks a piece of dirty blonde hair behind her ear.

"Maybe . . ." Missy says, smiling at Hannah.

I take another spoonful and almost choke on my yogurt. Missy is being so super-sweet to Hannah. If she thinks I believe for one second that she's not loving every minute of this . . .

"I can't wait to see my sketch," Jessica says, clutching her white dish of pomegranate with toasted almonds.

"Or what about when Colin sees you in it . . . ?" Taylor chimes in.

The prom talk continues, but I force myself to tune it out. Naturally, this only manages to make my thoughts return to Zachary. *What if I refuse his invitation and he goes with someone else? Would it be worse than if I say yes and he thinks that means that I forgive him? Maybe if I just go with him as friends . . .*

Finally, I just can't take it anymore. "Seriously? You guys are really letting Hannah design your prom dresses?"

Hannah grins proudly.

I shoot her a death stare.

"So, Kylie, are you in?" Jessica asks, elbowing me. "You should see the stuff Hannah is working on—it's amazing."

I scan my teammates. "For the last time, I'm good. Missy and I always shop together with our moms for our big day dresses. We've been doing it since like preschool graduation." I glance at Missy.

She looks down.

What I really want to say is I can't believe my teammates would trust someone who thinks that sewing mini Care Bears onto bags is fashion. (Not to mention the truth: that dress shopping is my mom's thing.)

Hannah nudges Missy with the magazine.

"What?" I say, annoyed that Hannah now thinks it's her responsibility to tell Missy when to talk.

Missy looks at Hannah out of the corner of her eye. "It's nothing," she says.

"No, what?" I ask, demanding an answer.

Again, they look at each other. And that's when it dawns on me: I know that look. People used to have it all the time when talking about Zachary. They know something that I don't.

Missy comes over to sit next to me. "Ky—please don't take this the wrong way—I actually have to wear a dress from our line. You know, to show off my marketing materials on my college app. So, I'm working on it with Hannah."

"What?!?"

"Before you freak, it's for college. I *have* to." She tugs at my jacket. "It's not like I *want* to."

I roll my eyes. "Whatever." I lean in and whisper, "You know you're going to look like a freak, right?"

"Ky, will you just trust me that I know what I'm doing?" Missy asks, her voice rising. Then she gets up and walks back over to Hannah, the magazine still in hand. "What cut are we going with for Tamika's neckline again?" she asks.

"A V-neckline," Hannah answers.

"Right. A V-neckline," Missy repeats, flipping through the magazine.

She's sucking Hannah for everything she can.

Tamika moves her arms like she's dancing. "I'm going to look so fine for senior prom this year and I didn't even have to worry about shopping."

"How do you know what to make?" Zoe asks Hannah.

"It's sketchy." She lets out a loud laugh. "Get it? Sketchy." She cracks herself up. "No, seriously. Somehow the ideas come to me and then one day it just meshes." Hannah shrugs her shoulders.

"So, is Vi letting you design her dress too?" I cut in.

Hannah breaks out in another fit of giggles. "Do skateboards fly?"

The group snickers.

"She's like you," Hannah says, lifting her nose in the air.

"And how's that?" I ask, daring Hannah to call me a snob.

She looks like she's about to take the bait when Jessica changes the topic. "So, what does Taylor's dress look like?" she asks.

"At first I was going with all white, but now I'm thinking a gray or a silver," Hannah says, crunching down on her Fruity Pebbles.

"But I totally trust Hannah." Taylor beams. "She'll know what works for me."

I roll my eyes. It's getting way too thick. I jokingly attempt to gag myself with my spoon. Abby and Zoe giggle.

Taylor, on the other hand, doesn't laugh. (Not that I'd expect her to.) But then she surprises me by slowly looking up at me, a newfound awareness in her eyes. "What's the deal, Ky? You seem so down. This isn't just about softball is it?"

I freeze, noticing that my hand has made its way to my heart pendant. Then I glare at her. She looks down and plays with her smoothie straw.

"Did something happen with Zach?" she whispers. This time she doesn't look up.

My teammates are stunned silent. Suddenly, the only sounds are the waves crashing against the sand and the squeak of Taylor's plastic straw.

Then Missy pipes up. "What are you talking about, Tay? Kylie hasn't spoken to Zach since their latest split." Missy nervously looks at me.

I glance at Zoe, silently begging her not to rat me out. Her eyes bug.

"Yeah, Kylie's over Zach," Tamika adds.

"They're done. . . . History," Jessica chimes in.

"Kylie?" Taylor asks. "Is that true?"

"Yeah, Ky. Is it?" Missy scooches closer to me from across the circle.

I survey my teammates, desperate for a way out of the conversation. But the more I try to come up with something, anything, to say, the more I realize there can only be one response. "Taylor's right. Zachary asked me to the prom."

thirteen

My teammates glance at one another frantically and then burst into a frenzy.

"Don't worry, girls. It's just an invite. Kylie would never go with Zach," Missy insists. "She's smarter than that."

"I'm sure she told him where to shove his invitation," Tamika adds.

"Yeah, Kylie would never give Zach a chance after the basketball season. I mean, what he did was . . ." Jessica pauses, scraping the bottom of her cup with her spoon. "Unforgivable."

I watch as my basketball buds chat about me like I'm not even there. *What do they know about Zachary and me?*

Eventually, I can't take it any longer. "Uh, hello. Earth to everyone, but we're talking about *my* life. *My* decision."

"You did tell him no, right?" Missy eyes me suspiciously.

"I didn't tell him yes, if that's what you want to know." I stand up, adjusting my jacket. Then I shove my napkins into my empty yogurt cup.

"Well, you'll show him when you get crowned prom princess," Abby says, smiling.

"Ooh, that'll be good," Missy agrees. "Win the crown, and then, while you're up on the stage, pick the hottest guy on the court—well, not Andrew—but the hottest guy, and hook up with him right there. In front of Zach."

"Ooh, what about Brett Davidson?" Eva suggests.

This sends the girls into a heated convo (again, about me!) and me into another mental freefall. I collapse back down. Prom princess. That's something that could turn this terrible year around. My mom would be so proud. Maybe she'd even come back home. Plus, Zachary would realize what he lost. And everyone would know that I'm more than just a washed-up benchwarmer.

"If you could have any guy at Beachwood, who would it be, Ky?" Jessica asks, interrupting my thoughts.

The answer pops into my head before I can stop it. But I can't exactly tell them that Zachary Murphy is my dream guy after they just spent the last few minutes plotting how to avenge my shattered pride. I decide to bounce.

"I'm out of here, chickies," I announce, standing up again.

"Wait. What? Where are you going?" Missy asks.

"Home." I shrug, dusting the sand off my shorts and bare legs.

"But . . ." Missy's face drops.

"Don't worry. I'll get a cab." I begin the trek toward the street, crossing over the bike path. Before getting too far, I remember the cup I'm clutching. I walk back to throw it away in the trash can at the edge of the beach, when I overhear Missy say, "I love Kylie and all, but I just don't get her anymore. I mean, why would she even talk to Zach after everything that happened? She can have any guy at Beachwood."

"I know," Tamika adds.

"It's so messed up. I don't get her either," Jessica says, pausing. "After everything he put her through . . ."

"I'm so worried about her." Missy shakes her head. "She's just going through so much. With the move and her parents' divorce. Why would she add Zach?"

My heart stops, and I begin to tiptoe away, glad no one's noticed that I've overhead their conversation. Then I break into a run. I smile as I sprint effortlessly down the bike path. But then, once I'm out of earshot, it occurs to me. Their conversation is still going on. Without me. And in that moment, reality hits me: I really am a benchwarmer, watching the world go by.

fourteen

I make it to the Shangri-La Hotel, when I realize that hailing a cab in LA is really as hard as people say. I decide to take a seat on a bench outside the hotel in the hopes that a cab will appear with some tourists in tow. *Not all of them are smart enough to rent a car, right?*

Fortunately, my strategy pays off. Just a few seconds later, a cab pulls up and an elderly couple emerges. I swiftly slide into the backseat.

"Where to?" the driver asks.

I hesitate and then give him Zachary's address. He nods at me in the rearview mirror and flips on the meter. I relax against the black leather and gaze out the window. Staring out, I spot a little girl with pigtails clutching a kite. Her parents stroll behind her, arms intertwined.

I'll never have that again, I think. An intact family. Two proud parents. A tribe. A tear forms in the corner of my eye and I wipe it before it can slip down my cheek.

I pull my phone out from my jacket pocket and scroll through to my mom's number.

Please. Please. Please pick up. I really need to talk to you right now.

"You have reached the voice mailbox of Catherine Collins. Please leave your name and a detailed message and I will return your call as soon as possible. Thank you for calling and have a nice day."

Figures.

"Mom, it's Kylie. I really need to talk to you tonight. Please call me back as soon as you get this message. Please."

I press "end" and notice that the cabdriver is looking at me strangely through his rearview mirror. I turn my head and take a few deep breaths. No more tears.

A few minutes later, the cab pulls up in front of the Murphy's mansion. I pay and climb out.

Trekking along the side of the house and through the wrought-iron gate, I sneak a quick peek at Zachary's window. Dark—figures. He's probably out with Vi. Traitor.

I let out a sigh and attempt to compose myself as I trudge through the wildflowers, past the cherry trees, through the garden, and across the gazebo. My dad bursts through the front door as soon as he spots me. His eyes are wide. "What are you doing? Are you okay? Did something happen?"

"Peachy." I shove past him and into our shack.

"I saw a cab drop you off. I thought you were with Missy," he says, his voice full of tension.

"I was. I decided to come home early."

"You could have called me. I would have picked you up."

"What, and interrupt yoga?"

"You know I don't host any yoga classes on Saturday nights. And besides, a cab is a waste of money." He follows me into the living room.

I swing around to face him, stopping in front of the bamboo side table. "It's not my fault we can't afford anything. I'm not the one who screwed up their marriage. You are."

His expression pains. "Kylie, I know you're under a lot of stress, but you're being unfair."

"Really? I'm the one being unfair? I'm not the person who refuses to use Mom's alimony for anything but necessary expenses."

"Ky, you know we still set aside money for your education."

"Thanks, Dad. That's swell of you. Really." I run my hand along the side table and spot my Under Armour softball bag lying beneath it. I quickly grab it and am about to begin the two-second walk to my room when my dad brings up the only topic that could make this worse.

"Your first game is right around the corner. I can't wait to see you play," he says, holding up a printout of my softball schedule.

"Where did you get that?" I ask. I feel my face burn.

"I printed it off your school website. Why?"

"Why . . ." I pause, searching for any excuse for why my dad shouldn't come to my games. I refuse to tell him that I lost the starting position. "Because you shouldn't assume that I'd want you to come to my games in the first place."

"Ky... I understand if you're mad at me, but your mother and I used to always see you play...."

"Exactly. You and *my mother*. But I don't see her here, do you? So, why don't we just make a clean break of it?" I lean over and pull out an empty plastic water bottle out of my bag. "Oops ..." I wiggle it in front of my dad.

His face turns red.

"Oh no ..." I toss the bottle on the Greenwood flooring. "Call the police! It's a plastic water bottle! Oh my God, I'm littering. Lock me up!"

"Oh, Kylie, I just don't know what to say to you anymore." My dad picks the water bottle off the ground.

"Nothing," I reply. "Just don't say anything at all." Then I stomp toward my room.

fifteen

Two and a half weeks later, I've pitched a total of zero innings. In fact, my butt is so warm from riding the pine that someone could roast marshmallows right off it. So much for being the backup.

"I still can't believe the junior prom is the same day as the Desert Invitational. What are you going to do?" Sophia, our third string pitcher, asks from her perch on the bench next to me.

"It's not really on my mind right now," I say grumpily as Chloe walks by me and sits on the other side of Sophia.

"Okay... So, what are you doing after today's game against Edgewater?" Sophia asks, her eyes wide.

"Huh?" I look her way.

"You know ..." She stares at her hands. "Are you hanging out afterward?"

"I'm just worried about softball right now. Not thinking about later. But thanks for asking."

Whatever.

I stand up and find a spot at the end of the bench as far away from Chloe and Sophia as possible. I know Sophia means well, but I just don't want Coach thinking I'm comfortable on the bench.

I stare out at the field. Phoenix and Nyla look bored—with Amber's amazing strikeout record, they've hardly had to do anything this whole game. Meanwhile, Amber drags dirt until the mound, the one that used to be mine, is perfect. Then she settles into her spot on the white rubber, takes a deep breath, winds up, and launches the ball. It smacks into Emily's glove with blazing speed.

"Strike," the umpire shouts.

The crowd—mostly parents and a few stragglers from other practices—explodes with cheers. A couple of guys from the lacrosse team, who just finished their practice at the field adjacent to ours, begin to chant Amber's name from center field.

Edgewater's number two steps out of the batter's box and glances at her coach, who waves off the signs. So much for signs, when Amber has struck out the other side three times.

Emily tosses the ball back to Amber and she begins to manicure her—*the*—mound again.

"No balls, one strike," the umpire announces.

Amber sets up, nods, and fires once more. A puff of chalk dust rises from Emily's glove.

The batter swings, but she's miles behind the pitch.

"Strike!" the umpire shouts again.

Whistles and cheers ring out from the crowd. A couple of B-Dubbers have even constructed blue *K* signs to mark

Amber's strikeouts. Eight are hanging on the center-field fence, not too far from where Chloe is standing. *They never did that for me.*

"Psst . . ." someone whispers into the dugout. I ignore it, figuring it's a freshman parent trying to sneak a snack in.

"Ky . . ." the person whispers.

I look over at the side opening of the dugout and spot Zachary behind the fence. He waves me over.

I stand up lazily and mosey over toward him. "Can't you see I'm busy?" I say.

"That should be you out there." Zachary points toward Amber.

I know. It should. I fight the urge to tell him how much I needed to hear that. "Yup. Sure," I say, feigning indifference.

"No really, Ky. I mean it."

"Whatever. What do you want?" I straighten up, watching Zachary's gaze hang on Amber a little too long for my comfort.

"Why do you always think I want something? Maybe I'm just here to cheer on my girl."

"Who? Amber?" I sneer.

He finally turns his gaze back to me. "Redheads don't really do it for me. I'm all about blondes." He reaches into the dugout and touches my hair.

I swat his hand away.

"Did you think any more about the prom?" Zachary looks down at me with his big chocolate eyes.

"Maybe," I say, remaining intentionally evasive. "Look, I got to get back to the bench. I have a lot of watching to do." I glance over at the coaches to see if they've noticed that their second string is chatting with a boy instead of focusing on the game.

They haven't. They're too busy writing down Amber's stats.

"You know I'm not going to take no for an answer." He grins.

"Well, you should have thought of that before you starting shoving your tongue down every B-Dub girl's throat," I sternly whisper. Amber's BFF, Danielle, glances at me from her spot on the bench. Her blue sparkly headband (Amber's sporting the same one today) glimmers from the afternoon sun.

I roll my eyes at her. She promptly returns the favor.

Whatever.

Then I continue in a whisper. "I'll never, ever, ever give you another chance. You're the one who screwed this up."

"Okay. Okay." Zachary holds up his hand in an attempt to get me to calm down. "I get it. You're mad. Then how about we just hang out as friends after your game. You look like you could use some Zach magic to cheer you up."

"No, I . . ."

"Not taking no for an answer. What time should I come over? I don't need much notice. I can be at your house in . . ." He smiles and pretends like he's trying to figure out a time. "Five seconds."

Oh for God's . . .

The crowd erupts as Amber sends another Edgewater girl back to the bench in defeat.

That's when I hear Coach Kate's voice rise above the din. "Wow! Did you see that rise ball? I haven't seen a pitcher throw a rise ball that hard since college!" Coach Kate proudly says to Coach Jackie.

Coach Jackie beams and nods. "Me either. Since senior year at UCLA."

My eyes begin to water.

I try to push the tears away and look at Zachary. "Fine. Just today. As friends. And don't you dare think it's anything more."

Zachary's face lights up just as my teammates jog in from the field, having successfully shut out the other team for another half inning.

"The guesthouse is still off-limits," I say, knowing if I keep giving in to him, that rule will bend like the rest.

"How about our spot?" Zachary asks, grinning.

"Fine."

"You know you love me."

The problem is I do.

sixteen

A few hours later, I grab Kibbles's leash off my desk and attach it to her collar. I take off toward Wavecatcher Beach to meet Zachary, my stomach twisting worse than the hairpin turns on Mulholland Drive.

Once outside, who should I spot but the very same Zachary Murphy scaling his front steps. He sees me and smiles. Kibbles pulls the leash toward him. I pull back.

"Not yet, Kibbles." Then I look at Zachary. "You need to go a different way."

"Can't we just walk together? We're going to the same place." He grins. He always thinks he can get whatever he wants with that smile.

"Nope," I say, pointing in the opposite direction.

"Fine." He hangs his head and shuffles down the street toward the beach. I turn around and take the long way.

Fifteen minutes later, I find myself staring at the infinite navy water, glistening beneath the setting sun. The sea breeze is cool tonight, but I welcome it after benchwarming all day. At least I'm up and moving. But I can't believe I'm moving toward Zachary.

I used to love this: Zachary, me, Kibbles, our spot. But that was before . . . *What was I thinking?*

"Thought you'd never get here," Zachary shouts. Still dressed in long mesh shorts and his Beachwood Academy blue Wildcat tee, he kept his promise (or at least one of them)—he's not treating this like a date.

Still, I'm breathing heavy and it's not from the walk.

Zachary grins, showing off his chiseled face, square chin, and deep dimple. "How's my girl?" he asks, stepping down from one of the two cliff seats at Wavecatcher Beach.

I cast a glance at the cliff and remember how we used to lie there, him tickling my stomach.

Kibbles does what I can't—she lunges playfully toward Zachary. As she charges forward, her tail thumps against the sand, spraying specks everywhere.

"Hey, Kibbles." Zachary squats down and rubs her head. Kibbles licks Zachary's face like it's an ice cream cone.

I tug back on her leash, but Kibbles won't budge.

Traitor.

After a few minutes of being smothered by Kibbles's kisses, Zachary turns his attention toward me. "I was hoping you'd come. I needed you." He takes a short step in my direction, his face inches from mine.

"I bet. . . ." This day has been tough enough. This was a bad idea. I should have never agreed to meet him.

I place my finger on Zachary's nose. I gently shove him back a few steps. "Remember, *friends* . . ."

"How can I forget? You still haven't responded to my prom invitation."

I shrug, beginning to really regret having come.

Zachary isn't dissuaded, but he has enough sense to change topics. "What's going on at softball?" He reaches down to pet Kibbles again, but I quickly pull back on her leash, this time successfully.

"Weren't you there today? You saw Amber on the mound."

"Yeah. So?"

"So? She had like a zillion strikeouts and her own personal cheering section."

Zachary takes another step toward me and grabs my arm. "That should be you. You should be the one out there.... Don't let it eat you up. Pretty soon, you'll be the one everyone is cheering for."

I look down at Zachary's hand. It feels so good to have it wrapped around my forearm. Just as comforting as it felt last September when he held me as I bawled my eyes out the night I learned about my parents' divorce.

I wiggle my arm from his grasp. I can't think like that. Zachary's not the person I thought he was.

"Ky, just please tell me what you're feeling...."

"I . . ." I look up into the chocolate speckles in his eyes and then, before I know what I'm doing, everything rushes out. "I just hate Coach Kate right now for picking Amber over me. Especially after everything I gave to the program." I let out a deep breath.

"Where did Amber come from anyway?" Zachary asks, cracking his knuckles.

I plop down onto the copper cliff seat and look up at the pink sky. "She's a transfer."

"Really?" Zachary raises his eyebrows and falls onto the cliff seat next to me. He's about to put his arm around me when Kibbles bounds onto my lap, ignoring Zachary.

"Good girl, Kibbles." I laugh.

Zachary shakes his head in mock disgust. "Seems like a no-brainer to me."

"What are you talking about?" I ask, stroking Kibbles's blonde fur.

"This whole starting spot mess," Zachary continues.

"Huh?"

"It's an easy fix. She transferred schools without a legit reason. She's an illegal transfer. Turn her in."

"She's not, though." I sit up.

"Who cares? Turn her in and let the CHSAA sort it out. In the meantime, you'll have playing time and she can ride the bench." Zachary jumps to his feet.

"I can't do that. Her parents got a divorce just last year." I shiver, pulling my softball warm-up tighter. Kibbles nudges between Zachary and me, her face resting on her paws. *I guess her loyalty was short-lived.*

"Yeah, so? What does that have to do with anything?"

"Only everything. I know how hard it is when your family is okay one day and *finito* the next. And plus, I only mess with girls who mess with you."

He snickers. "You're way too nice."

"Now that's definitely something I don't hear every day." I feel the sides of my mouth twitch into a grin.

"Then, I guess you have to hope that Amber chokes under all the pressure." Zach stares out at the dark ocean, then back at me. "Are you cold? You can borrow my jacket."

"I'm good." This whole mess would be so much easier if Zachary were mean to me. And even easier if Amber was. Then I could squash her.

"What's up? You know, since the move into the guest-house and everything . . ." Zachary looks at his hands. "Are you okay?"

"I'm fantabulous." I stare at the crashing waves. By now, the sun has set and the stars fill the sky like glitter.

"Have you heard from your mom?"

"Next question."

"Okay. How about . . . How's it going with your dad?"

Kibbles nudges Zachary's knee for more affection.

"If you call walking into Mr. SoCal Guru's makeshift yoga studio and finding a bunch of women in sweaty spandex suits bending and twisting all over my living room floor good, then it's going amazing." I pump my fist.

Zachary raises his eyebrows. "When are these classes?"

I shove him gently with my shoulder, keeping my arms glued to my side. "You would ask, you perv." Kibbles takes this as a sign that we like Zachary again. She stands up and nudges her nose in his shorts.

"Ha ha ha . . ."

"See, even Kibbles can't seem to keep her paws off you," I observe.

"What can I say? I'm irresistible." He shrugs his shoulders.

I shove him again.

Zachary falls over dramatically and erupts into laughter. Then, all of a sudden, he sits up, as if just remembering something.

"Yes . . . ?"

"I saw your dad the other day."

"What? When?"

"When I stopped by to see you."

Wait. Zachary stopped by to see me?

"You weren't there."

"It doesn't matter either way. I told you, the guesthouse is off-limits."

Zachary ignores me. "He gave me this green goopy drink. He told me it was algae or something. And that it'll help me with my joints."

"Urgh. The algae drink. It's one of his latest obsessions. Please tell me you didn't drink it."

"Of course I did. I'll do anything for basketball." Zachary flexes his bicep. "Can't you tell?"

I giggle. "Not exactly."

Zachary grins and lowers his arm. "Your dad's a good guy. He always means well."

"Yeah. My dad's great. He quit his job because he had a meaningless pain in his chest, 'realigned his priorities,' and chased my mom away. And now my mom has to work on the other side of the country just to 'start over' or to get away from him or for whatever reason she's doing it. And of course, my dad won't even take the money she makes." I cross my arms in front of my chest.

"I've known your dad since I was born. And trust me, he's a good guy. Better than . . ." Zachary stops himself.

"Yeah. Lucky for me that our dads were college roommates." I pump my fist again. "I didn't even have a chance at a normal life."

"The difference between your dad and my dad is your dad stopped partying after college and mine didn't," Zachary adds.

A chill runs up my back. "Did something happen tonight?" I ask. Without thinking, I reach my hand out to touch his arm. But then, in the last second, I pull back.

Catching me in the act, Zachary eyes me longingly. Then he breaks down. "The usual. I'm so sick of it. Dad was out drinking with his work buddies and then he came home all messed up. Mom and Dad were screaming at each other when I left."

"Was Zoe there?" I think about how many times Zoe,

Zachary, and sometimes even his mom used to sleep over in the guest bedroom of our old house after one of his dad's benders.

"Nope. She was still with you guys at practice. I texted her and told her to sleep at Abby's tonight." Zachary's eyes glisten. "I just can't take all the craziness anymore."

"I thought he was doing better." I smooth down Kibbles's fur.

Zachary rubs the top of his buzzed head. "Yeah. He was. Until he lost a deal at work last week. It's been downhill ever since." Zachary's hand falls to his side. "He's horrible to my mom . . . to us. I don't know why my mom continues to put up with his . . ."

"It'll pass. He'll get it back together. He always does. Maybe he'll go to rehab for real this time," I say. And then, before I realize what I'm saying, I ask, "Do you need to stay at my, uh, place?"

Zachary shakes his head. "I don't know what I'd do without you, Ky." He inches toward me.

"Hmm . . . Like half of Beachwood." I pull my legs up to my chest and balance on the cliff.

He stares at me for a second. Then he has an epiphany. "Enough of this," he exclaims. "It's time for some fun!" He rushes to his side of the cliff, pulls out two gloves, tosses one my way, and raises his arm like he's about to launch the ball from straightaway center field. "Go long!" he shouts.

I stand up and smack him in his rock solid gut with my

glove. Then I take off down the beach, shoving my left hand into the glove. I notice that the word BEACHWOOD is written in permanent marker across the palm. "Zachary Michael Murphy, where did you get these?"

"I snatched them after school. I'll put them back." He mischievously grins.

I shrug as Zachary tosses me the ball. I catch it effortlessly and stretch out my arm. Once I regain my footing, Zachary squats in front of me like a catcher.

"Okay, right here, Kylie." He punches the inside of the mitt. Then he sets up the glove.

I find a spot about forty feet away from Zachary, wind up, and fire, dragging my bare foot across the sand.

The ball smacks into Zachary's glove. "Strike one," Zachary shouts. "Not only is this girl beautiful, but she's an amazing pitcher." Zachary tosses the ball back to me.

I catch it, dig my foot into the sand, wind up, and fire again.

Smack.

"Ouch . . ." Zachary pulls out his hand and shakes it. "This girl throws some heat. Definitely UCLA bound if you ask me."

"Don't be such a baby."

"There's only one baby in my life." He winks. "And that baby can throw." He tosses the ball back to me. "Strike two."

As the sun begins to set, resembling an orange orb, I catch the ball and set up once again.

"Put her in the books."

I set up, whip my arm, and launch a fastball into Zachary's glove.

Pop.

"Man . . ." He tosses the glove onto the sand.

I jog over toward him. "Are you okay?"

"I've never seen a second string leave a catcher's hand looking like this." He shows me his red palm.

"I still got it!" I squeak. Then I proudly hold his bruised hand in mine.

seventeen

A few days later, I'm sitting in pre-calc, tracing the caramel swirls in my Caramel Frappuccino with my straw when my phone buzzes. With a flutter of anticipation, I pull out the phone from my back pocket, thinking that my mom is finally calling me back. Before anyone has a chance to notice, I quickly shove the phone underneath my desk for a peek.

FR: NICK
IS IT WARM IN HERE?

I let out a sigh, shove my phone back into my pocket, and take a sip of my Frap. The jokes about all the time I'm spending warming the bench are getting old.

"Since we still seem to be having problems with logarithmic functions, I'd like you to work together in groups of three today," Mrs. Cunningham says. She scrawls the even problem numbers on the board.

As I'm pulling my desk next to Missy's, taking care not to spill my drink, Nick steps next to me. "You didn't answer me. Is it warm?"

Nick laughs and holds up his hand for a high five to Andrew.

"Don't even." Missy glares at Andrew.

He lowers his arm.

Nick holds his hand up to Brett, who freezes. "Don't get me involved." He looks at me.

I hold his gaze.

"Is there a problem, Mr. Solerno?" Mrs. Cunningham asks.

"No, Mrs. Cunningham." Nick grins.

I wink at Brett and fall next to Missy. "You'll never guess who I met at the beach."

Missy continues to furiously mock up a Banana Fad brochure in her sketchbook. "Please tell me it was Brett Davidson. I saw the way you guys were just looking at each other. . . . Yummy." She lets out a long breath and changes her angle. Then she continues to shade.

"Zachary showed up at my game. . . ."

Missy stops shading, but doesn't look at me directly. "Please tell me you did not fall off the wagon again."

Phoenix comes over, interrupting our conversation. "Can I work with you guys?" she asks.

I glance at Missy to see if she cares, but she's already resumed her shading. Even though I want to finish our convo about Zachary, I shrug and say, "Sure." Then I point to the empty desk next to us.

Hannah drags a desk over to our group. She plops *Prom* magazine on top of Missy's desk.

The edge of the magazine lands on Missy's sketchbook. Immediately she pops her head up. "Ohmigod!" she squeals. "Is that the magazine with *the* dress? You know the one with the black lace?" she asks, breathless.

"Yeah. It's sick," Hannah says. Her soda tab bracelets clang against the desk.

"I've been dying to see this dress. . . ." Missy exhales, frantically paging through the magazine. "I think it's just the perfect inspiration for the marketing campaign."

"Uh—excuse me," I butt in. I can't let Hannah get any ideas about staying put. "Looks like we're full. Mrs. Cunningham said three today." I reach over and pull Phoenix's desk closer toward mine.

"Shhh . . . Ky," Missy whispers. "Maybe if we don't say anything, Mrs. Cunningham will make an exception."

Before I can open my mouth, I'm distracted by the sound of a scrunched-up paper ball being deflected by a pre-calc textbook. Judging by the look of it, the ball was on its way toward us before Amber's BFF Danielle stopped it with her book. *Great, now I owe her one.*

"Nice try, Nick," she says. She lowers her book and continues to work with Sophia.

"Wow. Do you ride the pine with Kylie too, Danielle? With that kind of talent on the bench, I can't imagine what's on the field." Nick chuckles. "Maybe you guys will win one more game than last year. That would make you like four and fourteen, right?"

Danielle pipes up. "I don't know how you people stand each other. Your whole group is *so* immature." She looks at Missy, Nick, Andrew, and Brett, her eyes landing on me.

"And tie-dyed socks are just the model of maturity?" I say to Danielle. I pick the paper ball up off the floor and toss it back at Nick.

Nick ducks and the paper ball nails Andrew in the head. They both crack up.

"Deserved." Missy pops her head up from the magazine.

"What did I do?" Andrew holds up his hands.

"Wait," Hannah says. She jumps up on top of my desk like it's a skateboard.

"What the . . ." I'm face-to-face with Hannah's hot pink Chucks.

"See that?" She points to the black-and-white *The Wisdom of Albert Einstein* poster hanging above the whiteboard.

Missy and I, stunned silent by Hannah's eccentric behavior, can't help but look up at the poster. For once, we're both thinking the same thing: *What could Hannah possibly see in that poster of Einstein, besides wild eyes and frizzy hair?*

"Yeah?" I ask, shocked that Mrs. Cunningham hasn't looked up from grading papers to put an end to Hannah's spectacle.

"It's perfect!" she shouts, pointing at the poster. She jumps down off the desk. "It's exactly what I needed to finish Eva's dress. The whites and the black . . ." She gazes off.

"Uh . . . We're in class . . ." I begin to say.

"Psst . . . Ky," Brett Davidson whispers behind me.

I roll my eyes at Hannah and turn around to enjoy some eye candy.

He moves his long dark bangs away from his eyes and looks up at me sheepishly.

In that second, I feel a little bad for ignoring Brett lately—I of all people should recognize when someone is just trying to save face in front of their friends. "Brett , I'm . . ."

"No, Ky, me first." He pauses. "I was wondering if you've . . ."

Two beeps silence the class.

"Hello?" A voice from the main office echoes through the wall speaker, interrupting the chaos.

"Yes!" Mrs. Cunningham jumps up from her spot at the desk.

"Could you please send Kylie Collins to Coach Kate's office?"

"Sure!" Mrs. Cunningham scans the room. "Kylie. Kylie Collins?"

"Maybe you'll actually play a few innings today," Nick says to me as I stand up. "JV, that is."

I glance at Nick. "The day I'll play JV softball is the day you'll actually get a girlfriend."

Brett and Andrew chime in, "Aww, man! Good one."

I concentrate on Brett. "Talk later?"

"Definitely." His dark eyes hold on to mine. He nods and leans back on his chair.

As I slowly begin the walk toward Coach Kate's office, I wonder what Brett could have had to say to me that was so important. But then, as I hit the phys ed hallway and walk past the trophy case filled with accolades from every sport except softball, my thoughts turn to Coach Kate: *Why on earth is she calling me into her office? It's probably not to tell me that she's sorry for completely ruining my life.*

I pick up the pace and make the right toward Coach's office. When I reach her door, I suck in my breath and attempt to calm the butterflies. Nick's voice echoes in my head. *Could he be right? Is this about demoting me to JV?* That'd be even worse than warming the bench.

I console myself by thinking about what a jerk Nick is—he doesn't know anything. Then I steady my nerves and tap on Coach Kate's wooden door.

"Come in," she yells from inside. As I walk toward her, the Frap I just devoured swishes around in my stomach. I look over at Martie's door at the other end of the hallway. How is it that just three short months ago I was inside her office hashing out the Taylor Thomas and Zachary Murphy mess, and now here I am again? Well, not in Martie's office per se, but in a similarly hellish situation.

I peek inside Coach's office. She's scanning our local newspaper, the *Beachwood Sun*, and furiously scribbling on a pad of paper. Her platinum hair is tight at the base of her neck.

"Kylie," she says, glancing up. "Thanks for coming. Have

a seat." She motions to the gray fabric chairs in front of her desk.

"Hey, Coach," I answer, nervously sliding into the chair closest to the door. "Anything good?" I nod at the newspaper in an attempt to stall for time.

"Just looking through the stats from the weekend. Seeing how the other teams in our conference are stacking up. Eyeing Santo Bay. You know the drill."

I nod. I do. It's something I also do obsessively.

Coach leans back on her leather chair. "I called you in this afternoon to tell you that Amber is home with strep throat. You'll be starting today."

"What?" I hold on to the sides of the chair like it might take off and fly around the office.

Coach sits up suddenly. Then she leans in close, as if she's just now decided it's time for us to have an overdue heart-to-heart. "Look, I know this season has been extremely difficult for you, Kylie. It's not easy to watch someone take your position away. A position that you worked really hard to win."

For a second, I feel bad for all the horrible things I've said about Coach Kate. She's not really a spineless freak. She's just doing what's best for the team. And pretty soon, she'll realize that what's best for the team is . . . ME.

"Thanks, Coach," I say, standing up.

"It'll be nice to see you take the mound again." She stands up with me. "I'll see you in a few."

Yup, you will, I think. *And when you do, you'll have no choice but to give me my spot back.* I calmly walk out of her office. Then I release the breath I hadn't realized I'd been holding. *Normal. Everything is going back to normal.* I reach up and grab my heart charm, rubbing the white gold between my index finger and thumb.

eighteen

About three hours later, at the top of the seventh inning, the infielders—including Phoenix, Nyla, Abby, Jessica, and *ME*—gather at the mound and shout, "Beachwood!"

"Academy!" the outfield echoes, and disperses to their positions.

"Nice work." Nyla gently taps me on the back with her glove.

"Kylie's back!" Abby shouts.

Jessica adds, "Kylie's not just back. Kylie's a beast!"

"I know! Talk about *devouring* the competition!" Phoenix yells.

I burst into a huge grin at that one. It feels so good to be back inside our complex with the girls—and not as a stupid, insignificant onlooker.

"Balls in," the umpire calls from his spot behind home plate.

Nyla hands me the ball and smacks my leather glove. "Go get 'em, Killer Ky."

I smile even wider. "Killer Ky" is the understatement of the century. Bel Air hasn't scored in six innings. Meanwhile, our team is up by two, and I've earned five strikeouts and no walks. We're in the perfect position to continue our winning streak—if we win today, we're undefeated with five wins. And that moves us into serious consideration for the Desert Invitational and that much closer to saving the softball program.

I tuck my glove in between my knees and shove my shiny white number seven home jersey into my matching shorts. Then I reach down and pull up my socks. When I'm finished, I fill a little dirt into a small hole that's appeared in front of the rubber from Bel Air's pitcher. Although I've never been one to manicure my mound, it seems to work for Amber, so I continue to smooth out the rest.

"First batter," Coach Kate yells from the dugout. "Nyla, your way twice."

"Batter up!" the umpire shouts as Zoe settles in behind the plate. Since Emily sprained her wrist, Zoe took over her spot at catcher and has been doing amazing.

"Go, Kylie!" Zachary shouts from the stands.

I feel an extra little spring to my step. As much as I love Zoe, I secretly suspect that Zachary is only here to watch me. *Not that I would ever tell her that . . .*

My self-congratulatory moment ends as soon as I see Bel Air's number fourteen set up at the left side of the plate. It's time to focus.

"Watch the drag," I shout at my teammates, turning around so that all of them can hear me. I spot the four *K* signs hanging in center field to mark my strikeouts—five if you include the giant blue *K* painted on Brandon's chest. (Apparently, the lacrosse guys didn't have enough poster board for all of my strikeouts.) The smile on my face grows to enormous proportions—Amber isn't the only one who gets the star treatment.

As I turn to face the Bel Air batter, I can feel Jessica to my left and Phoenix to my right inching toward the batter's box. They have the right idea—the last thing we need is a batter on. I set up on the rubber and take a deep breath. Zoe gives me the first sign—a fastball, tight and inside. I glance toward first base and make eye contact with Jessica. She reads my expression and inches up even closer. Confident that my teammates are in position, I feel for the C-grip, wind up, take a huge step, and snap the ball hard.

Fourteen explodes out of the batter's box, dragging her bat through the strike zone.

Dong.

The ball hits the inside of the bat and rolls slowly toward Jessica, who's in front of the bag. She picks it up bare-handed and fires it to first. Abby sprints from second to the bag and covers first just in time.

Instantly, the crowd erupts.

From the dugout, our subs Sophia and Chloe look on in awe. Danielle just glares.

"Out," the field umpire shouts.

I pump my fist. There's no way Amber's coming back after this performance.

"One out," Nyla yells, holding up one finger as she receives the ball from the infield toss around. She jogs it to me, drops it into my glove, and slaps hands.

I look around the field, glancing over at the stands. Zachary's still seated at the top of the bleachers, smiling at me. To his far left, Hannah and Missy wave at me, and Taylor gives me a thumbs-up.

I can do this. Just two more outs and I have a future in softball—at Beachwood AND maybe even at UCLA.

Bel Air's second batter digs in. I recognize her immediately. Two innings ago, she launched my fastball hard toward left field.

Zoe gives me the sign. Fastball outside. I shake her off. She gives me another—changeup. *Perfect.*

With my hand hidden inside my glove, I bend my fingers and grip the knuckle change. Then I wind up and fire. The ball barely makes it over the plate.

The batter is miles ahead of it. So much so, she could have swung twice.

"Strike one," the umpire calls.

Again the crowd erupts.

Zoe fires the ball back to me. Then she sets up inside and gives me the screwball sign. *Ahh, too easy.*

I rearrange the dirt (Amber's strategy seems to be working) and set up. I move my thumb to the bottom of the C-grip, wind up, stride to the left, and twist my wrist, peeling the ball into a perfect right tight spiral.

The Bel Air batter half swings and jams herself.

Dong.

The ball ricochets off the inside of her bat, so close it almost hits the grip, and rolls to a stop a foot in front of Zoe. She rips the catcher's mask off her face and fires the ball to Jessica at first.

"Out!"

"One more out, B-Dub!" the crowd shouts.

My teammates once again toss the ball around the horn. When the infield is finished, Nyla hands me the ball and yells, "Two down. Go to first!" Then she returns to her position at short.

Number twenty-three digs into the batter's box. *She's the only one who has two hits off me today.*

"Your way, Nyla and Phoenix!" Coach Kate calls out from the dugout.

Our bench begins to yell, "Hey, batter take a hike! 'Cause Kylie's gonna pitch a strike!"

Unlike my ASA team, Beachwood Softball hasn't sung dugout cheers since long before I joined. And I'm loving every minute of it.

Zoe shows four fingers. Another screwball. I definitely want to end this game the way I've been winning it, with my go-to pitch. Amber might have the rise, but she doesn't have my screwball.

I wind up and release the ball.

Number twenty-three doesn't move. The pitch cuts right at the perfect time.

"Strike," the umpire shouts.

"Woot!" The stands burst into cheers.

"Kylie is a friend of mine. She can strike you out any-time!" the bench cheers.

I puff out my chest and dig my royal-blue spike into the mound. I set my feet on the rubber. Fastball outside. I shake it off. Zoe gives another sign for a curve. I shake her off once again.

Twenty-three holds up her back hand in the stop position and steps out of the batter's box.

"Time," the umpire calls.

I step off the rubber and wait for twenty-three to dig in again. I hate it when batters call time to slow down the pace of the game. So stupid.

Once the batter digs in again, Zoe shows two fingers. I shake her off. She knows I want to throw the screwball. She shows me four fingers.

I wind up and throw the screwball again.

Twenty-three isn't fooled. She makes contact, but fouls the ball over our dugout.

"Foul ball," the umpire yells. "No balls and two strikes."

"Straighten it out!" the other team shouts. They stand in a row at their dugout fence, knowing this is their last chance.

"Put her away, Kylie," Coach Kate screams from our dugout.

Bel Air's dugout roars.

Zoe gives me a screwball sign, but I shake her off this time. Number twenty-three is on to me. She holds out five fingers. The rise ball. I freeze.

If I throw the rise ball and blow it, I'm sure Coach will reinstate Amber. But if I shake Zoe's sign, Coach will know my rise is still weak and might go with Amber anyway.

I stare at Zoe's fingers, trying to will myself into action. She gives me the sign again.

I can't help myself. I shake her off.

"Time," Zoe says to the umpire. She removes her mask and jogs to the mound. "What's up?"

"Change," I say into my glove so the Bel Air batter doesn't read my lips.

"She's expecting that." Zoe holds her catcher's mitt in front of her face. "You've been messing with batters all day with the change."

"Then screwball it is, freshman," I say to Zoe.

"Your call." Zoe shrugs.

Zoe turns around and jogs back to position. She maneuvers into her squat. Then she gives me four fingers.

I wind up and fire.

I thought twenty-three was smarter than the rest, but I gave her way too much credit. I let go of the pitch too soon and she chases a high ball out of the strike zone.

"Strike three." The umpire punches the air.

The complex explodes into cheers.

Nyla smacks me on the back.

Jessica follows. "Way to go, Ky!"

"Yeah, Ky. Nice job!" Abby beams.

"You rock," Phoenix adds on her way by.

I stand on the mound for a minute and let it all soak in. Then I scan the crowd. Zachary is on his feet cheering. Taylor, Missy, and Hannah are literally jumping up and down. My teammates continue to scream my name. At last, everything is back to normal.

Ignoring the roar of the complex, I close my eyes and picture myself two years from now: I'm standing on the mound at UCLA's Easton Stadium wearing a crisp white, pale blue, and pale yellow short uniform. Just like now, the crowd is on their feet. I've just struck out the side. And Amber is a distant memory . . .

nineteen

A half hour later, I'm still floating. Seriously. My feet are literally ten feet off the ground.

I duck into the team room to call my mom to share news of the amazing game when Nyla smacks me on my back again, landing right on my number seven jersey.

"Wow! Kylie! Way to go," Emily shouts, her wrist in an Ace bandage.

"Amazing game!" Zoe adds.

Chloe and Sophia look like they're about to say something too when Coach Kate walks in, followed by Assistant Coach Jackie. "Nice screwball today," she says. Mimicking Nyla, she pats me on the back.

I'm golden. My spot is mine again.

"Okay, everyone, grab a seat on the benches," Coach Kate announces. She rests the score book up against the whiteboard as Jessica runs in, looking harried.

Guess she got caught talking to Colin.

We find our spots on the vertically aligned wooden benches. Nyla and Phoenix shove next to me. The rest of the team files behind us. Without turning around, I feel more than see my other teammates trying to grab my attention. (Meanwhile, Danielle sits as far away as possible.)

But before I can even say "thanks" (to everyone but Danielle, of course), Coach launches into her speech. "As many of you know, we're gearing up for the annual Desert Invitational tournament. And with another win today that places us at the number two seed, behind Santo Bay. There's no way the Board of Trustees will demote us to club status with this effort! Beachwood Academy Softball will have a long life as an interscholastic sport if we keep up our intensity."

My teammates burst into cheers. If I thought I was having a hard time keeping my feet on the ground before, it's nothing compared to the way I feel now. *Coach essentially just said that I saved the day.*

For a moment, I'm in heaven.

But then I notice the fiery determination in Coach's eyes, and I realize it's not over yet.

"Incredible outing against Bel Air today. I was so impressed with our teamwork, communication on the field, and overall performance." Coach eyes me as she grins. "Kylie's amazing game on the mound was just what we needed."

I was right. I'm so the number one starter.

"But we're just at the beginning of the biggest fight in Beachwood history. It's time to bring it up another notch. And to take the momentum of today into tomorrow and the rest of the week."

Coach pauses and I can't help it—I wonder if the other shoe is about to drop.

It does.

"And with Amber's presence, we're unstoppable!"

Did Coach just mention Amber the same day I pitched the greatest game of my life?

"It's our turn! We're going to bring home our first Beachwood Academy banner in almost a decade. With all this effort, we might even come away with the district title."

Everyone cheers again, except for me. It's like no one even noticed what just happened.

"Get a good night's sleep and be ready for practice tomorrow." Coach grabs her scorebook from the whiteboard edge. "I'll see you then."

Did she seriously just say that?

I wait until my teammates vacate the team room, then barrel up to Coach Kate, interrupting her conversation with Coach Jackie. "Can I talk to you for a second?" I ask.

To Coach Jackie she says, "Why don't you meet me in my office in five minutes?" And then to me, "Yes, Kylie?"

"I just wanted to double check what you meant when you mentioned Amber." I shift nervously.

Coach's eyes narrow. "What do you mean?"

"I just thought that after the game today you would see that I'm the one who should be starting." I pause for a second and then I let it all out. "You saw my screwball today. I dominated Bel Air. And you know how important Division I is to me. It's all I . . ." I stop myself when I see Coach Kate's bottom lip jut out just a bit. And before I sound just plain pathetic.

Coach Kate's shoulders slump. "I'm sorry, Kylie. I know this is really hard. And I know we've been working together for a number of years . . ." She lets out a breath. "But you know, Santo Bay isn't Bel Air. They're not the same team. Have you been working on your power and the accuracy of your rise ball?" She tilts her head to the side.

I face her head-on. "Of course I have. And you know it's not all about the rise ball. I have movement on my pitches. Accuracy. My screwball."

Coach Kate crosses her arms. "You're a very good control pitcher, Ky, and I'd love for you to start again. But with Amber's rise ball being over sixty-five miles per hour, how can I possibly bench her? Without that kind of power in your arsenal, I just can't permanently move you to the starting spot."

"But that spot was mine for—"

Coach Kate interrupts me. "I know, Kylie. That spot was yours for two years. And I can only imagine how this must hurt you. But you know as well as I do that this is the best thing for the team."

"I—" I cut myself off when I feel the hot tears start to build. The problem is Coach Kate is right. I turn around and sprint out of the team room.

twenty

I push off the rubber again and again and again. This time the stands are silent. Everyone else went home two hours ago, but I'm still here, standing on the same rubber I just pitched the best game of my life off of two hours ago. *Little good that did.*

I push off again. Before I release, I twist my hand like I'm opening a door and attempt to bring forward as much power as I can muster from my legs. *I can do this. I can throw a rise ball as hard as Amber.*

The ball thumps against the padded fence. I grab another ball out of the royal-blue bucket and look up at the pink sky, wiping the sweat off my forehead. As I do so, the wind picks up, sending a chill through my white number seven jersey. But I'm not stopping. Not until I get it right.

The first thing I did after Coach Kate criticized me for not playing as well as Amber was text Coach Malone to ask for some additional sessions. The second was to come out here. If Coach Kate doesn't think I work hard enough, I'll show her.

I push off the mound again and the ball tails up.

Thump.

Still not hard enough. Still too high.

I reach into the bucket and grab another ball.

Explode off the mound recites in my head. Words Coach Malone uses over and over. *Use your hips. It's all in the legs.*

I push off again.

Thump.

Still not hard enough.

I bend down to grab another ball from the bucket.

"Hey, hottie!" someone catcalls from the stands.

Since it's not the first time I've been heckled, I ignore it. I don't have time for silly games.

I wind up and fire as hard as I can.

Thump.

Damn.

My arm is heavy. So heavy, it feels like it's been dipped in concrete. I wipe the sweat off my brow again. When I do, my fingers tingle.

"Ky!"

This time I look over at the stands.

Zachary.

I quickly wave, bend over, and grab another ball out of the bucket. I don't have time for him right now.

"Why are you working so hard? You just nearly pitched a no-hitter," he yells.

I shrug and stare at the bucket next to me. "I don't have time to talk." I grab another ball.

Zachary must realize that this strategy isn't going to work because he jogs out toward the mound. "Ky," he says, grabbing my arm.

I can't help myself—I look up. And... butterflies. Even in black mesh shorts and a sweat-stained gray Beachwood Academy Basketball tee, Zachary sends flutters through me. I pull my arm from his grasp.

"Don't you think you should take a break? This can't be good for your arm."

"Why do you care? You always say you don't like softball."

"Don't you mean cotton ball?" he jokes.

"Really? Like that's going to win my heart. Don't you have a freshman girl to go kiss for points?" I accidentally on purpose throw the ball at Zachary's abs.

He catches it. Then he walks up to me, making as if he's going to hand the ball back. But as he's about to reach me, he whispers, "There's only one girl I want to be kissing...."

"Shut up." I jokingly push Zachary away. "How about you set up in the batter's box? That way I can strike you out. I could use the pick-me-up."

Zachary puffs out his chest like a peacock. "You never strike me out."

I roll my eyes. "Yes, I do. I've done it like a hundred times, and you know it."

"A hundred times?" he asks, taking note of my exaggeration. His brown eyes twinkle.

"Well, maybe not a hundred times, but you know what I mean." I playfully push him again.

Zachary steps in front of me, placing his hands on my shoulders. "Look, I came to your game today because I know how much you care about the starting position."

"Guess you're the only one..."

"*A*, that's not true. And *B*, even if it were, come on, we've always been there for each other." He pauses. "You just helped me get through all the stuff with my dad the other day."

"That was different. That was..."

"No, that was *us*. That's what we do." He gently rubs my cheek with the back of his hand.

The thing is he's right: it is. I remember how Zachary was the only one there for me three years ago when my mom just "had" to go away during an ASA tournament. And when the first cracks in my parents' marriage began appearing. And when...The memories are too numerous to count.

Zachary senses I'm getting lost in my thoughts. "It was great to see you out there again," he says, smiling.

I'm melting.

"And I know how much all this means to you."

I'm a puddle.

"You've been working so hard at cotton ball since you were a kid." He gives me a playful knock on the chin.

"You were doing okay until you mentioned cotton ball." I pick up the bucket and begin to carry it toward the team room.

Zachary tries to grab the bucket from me.

I don't let go. "What? Do you think because I'm a girl I can't carry the ball bucket?"

Zachary shrugs. "Nah, I just thought a little chivalry might win you over. Speaking of which, are you going to the prom with me or what?"

I hold my hand to my heart in mock rapture. "How can I refuse an invitation like that? So well thought out and with such concern for me? Wow. You're such a romantic, Zachary Murphy."

Zachary smirks. "I make up for it with my good looks . . . and other natural abilities. . . ." He jabs me in my side, winking.

"Whatever." I wiggle away from his touch. "Race you to the team room!"

I sprint as fast as I can before Zachary even has a chance to realize what's happening. The grass crunches beneath my feet. Even though I have a head start, I can feel him gaining behind me. Finally, I pull open the door to the team room with every ounce of strength I possess. That's when I see a blur rush past me. My arm suddenly feels light. I look down. The bucket is gone.

"Beat ya!" Zachary calls out. He's placed the bucket where it belongs.

"That's because you cheated!"

"So did you!"

"Come on," he says, pulling me along.

We tread back across the field, giggling along the way. I look up at the stars now glimmering in the dark sky and press my index finger to my chin. "Hmm . . . Let me think about the invite."

"You know you want me." Zachary chuckles.

"You're making this really easy . . ." I tease.

"You and me, babe."

"Ah. No." I smile and begin to jog ahead of him. "Rematch?"

Zachary yells to me. "I don't know what you're running away from. You live in my backyard."

I laugh and pick up my pace.

"I'm not giving up on you yet," he shouts. "And I would still look into Amber's transfer if I were you."

"Whatever," I yell, jogging backward. "Don't worry about me and cotton ball anymore. We're doing just fine."

twenty-one

I stand in front of my bedroom mirror, fiddling with a series of pretend updos for prom exactly two weeks before the big night. Not that I've decided to go with Zachary or anything. But just because prom is supposed to be "the most special moment of a young woman's life," or so my mom says. And I figure it can't hurt to prepare.

I'm interrupted by the buzzing of my phone. I check the screen. Missy.

"I'm parked out front of that house where I've been dropping you off. But it's dark. What gives?"

"Uh. Uh. I'm not there. . . ."

"Whatever. Anyway, want to check out prom dresses with me tonight in Beverly Hills? I'm in desperate need of some inspiration for the marketing ideas I'm working on. I can't let Hannah take credit for everything now that Banana Fad is taking off."

Ugh. I balance the phone against my ear and peek out the guesthouse window. Zachary's room is dark. He left me an hour ago to work out.

I should have skipped playing with my hair and spent the time practicing my pitching.

Meanwhile, Missy continues to babble. "I need to hit the stores stat and brush up on my fashion." She lets out a dramatic sigh in my ear.

With everything that's been going on lately, I'm tempted to tell Missy that I wish her and Hannah a happy life together. But then I think, what would Vi say about my staying home on a Saturday night?

After all, the last Saturday night Vi saw me out, she thought I was pretty lame to be grabbing frozen yogurt. And it's not like I've been out much lately.

I pretend to catch my breath. "Look, I'm out running. Meet me on the corner of Beach and Driftwood."

"See ya in two," Missy says, and hangs up.

Quicker than Amber can say rise ball, I don full running gear. I pull my hair up in high ponytail, replace my skinny jeans with black Nike shorts, and pull a white Henley over my tank. Then I slide on my running shoes, shove my white iPod buds in my ears, and run into the bathroom to throw some water (aka instant sweat) on my face. I manage to sneak out the door before Dad even notices.

I take off down the street, sprinting as fast as I can, and pull the brakes at the stop sign.

A few seconds later, headlights flash across my face as Missy pulls up in her black BMW.

She rolls down the window when she spots me. A breeze of Dior perfume hits my nose.

"What are you doing, Sporty Spice?" Missy asks. "It's Saturday night."

I rest my hands on my knees, pretending to be out of breath. "You can never be too in shape," I say, faking heavy breathing.

She unlocks the passenger side door.

"Forget something?" Missy pulls a pink petal out of the back of my ponytail as I settle into the passenger side. She shows it to me. "Don't Zach's parents have cherry trees in their backyard?"

"Oh . . . it must have been the wind. And what, are you a botanist now?" I grab the petal and toss it out the window.

"Please tell me this didn't come from Zach's place." Missy stares at me, her mouth wide open.

"No, I already told you. I was running. And the wind must have carried it over." I smooth down the back of my hair, trying to root out any straggling petals.

"Nice try, Super Fly." She tilts her head. "And anyway, why would you be rolling around Zach's backyard when you could be macking it with Brett Davidson?"

"I don't know why you always bring Brett up. It's not like he's into me."

"Not into you? Kylie Collins, do you see the way he looks at you?"

"Yeah, like: *Can you please help me with my math homework?*"

"More like: *Can you please have my babies?*"

I pause, thinking about whether there could be any truth to what Missy's saying. He did try to talk to me the other day. . . . But then I realize the obvious response. "If he likes me so much, then why hasn't he asked me to prom?"

"Maybe because you're always shooting death rays from your eyes." Missy does an impression of me.

"Ugh, seriously, Miss? Now, you're just making things up."

"Ky . . ." she says, her eyes narrowing.

"Okay, so maybe I have been a little standoffish lately."

Missy bursts out laughing. "I don't even know where to begin with that one. A little? Standoffish? Lately?"

"Very funny. So, what shops do you want to hit tonight on your so-called quest for fashion inspiration?" I ask, attempting to change the subject.

Missy sees right through me. "Maybe we should start with you telling me what's really going on between you and Zach."

I look at the window so that my eyes can't give me away. As much as I want to tell her the truth, I can't risk her blabbing to Hannah. "There isn't anything to tell," I say.

Missy lets out a loud breath. "Whatever," she says. Then she hits the gas and merges onto the Pacific Coast Highway.

A few hours later, Missy has decided to ignore my indiscretions and focus on the matter at hand: clothes. "I'm loving this one," she says, pointing to an electric minidress. "I just adore the color."

"Yeah, it's great," I say, sipping the Frappuccino I just bought with a gift card. To distract myself, I pull out the straw and lick off the whip cream—thanks to my dad's stupid rules, I won't be buying any items during today's excursion. Apparently, I have "more clothing than any girl my age could possibly need."

"Can you believe the pre-prom assembly is this Monday?" Missy says, pulling her sketchbook out from her oversized Tory Burch bag. "It's crazy to think that prom is actually almost here."

My Frap crawls up my throat. "I know. We've waited our whole lives for this. . . ."

"Remember when we used to lie on your bed and talk about who we were going to go with and what we were going to wear and how we were going to be on prom court and . . ."

Under my breath, I say, "And how we were going to go shopping with our moms . . ."

Missy hears me anyway. "Yeah, I know. Isn't it funny how things work out?" she exclaims. "Who would have thought that I'd end up part of a design team?"

"Not me," I say, snidely.

Missy doesn't catch my tone. "Not me either!"

I decide to play nice. "Well, you always knew who you'd be going with. Right?"

She looks guilty, but she doesn't say anything.

Missy's not budging, so I decide to change the subject.

"You're so going to make prom court on Monday," I say, biting my bottom lip.

A new expression appears on Missy's face. Excitement. "Hello?" she says. "We're totally going to be on it together. Like the eighth grade Snow Ball and Toddlers & Tiaras. Remember the pageants?"

I release my lip. "Pageants weren't my thing."

"They were your mom's thing." She grins, but then frowns. "Sorry. How is the mom?"

"Don't want to talk about it." I pick my Frap off the table and sip the last of it.

"Gotcha." Missy pulls the drink from my grasp.

As she does, I realize that I've been mindlessly scraping the bottom of the cup with my plastic straw.

She places her sketchbook back into her bag and ushers me out of the store. "Okay, so then let's just forget about Mommy Dearest for a second and say that you're so going to win prom princess."

We step out onto Robertson Boulevard and I turn to face Missy. "Miss, I appreciate the pep talk and everything, but we both know that given recent events . . ." I pause.

Missy uses this as an opportunity to interject. "If you're about to say that you're not going to get prom princess because of some silly softball position and Z—"

"Some silly softball position?" This time it's my turn to cut her off. "You didn't think basketball was silly."

She throws my empty cup into the nearest recycling bin.

"You know I didn't mean it like that. I just said *you* should be prom princess. I'm on your side."

Oh yeah, she's really on my side.

Missy sees that I'm still seething and tries to change tactics. She points to a vintage pink dress visible through a store window. "You would look amazing in that color."

"Miss, don't try to butter me up," I say, crossing my arms.

"No, really." She pulls her sketchbook back out and jots down a few notes. "I'd love to work with Hannah to design a dress like that for you." She shuts her book.

I let out a deep breath. "Honestly, Miss . . ." I pause. "It's not about the dress. Or even just about softball. I have other stuff. . . ."

Missy shoves her book back into her bag and looks at me with concern. "Like what? Like Zach? Like living in someone's guesthouse?"

"It's not about the house either . . ." I say.

She freezes. "Is it about the big D?"

"Sort of." I take a deep breath. "I just want to go shopping with my mom. Since she's moved to Manhattan, she's never around and I figured shopping for a prom dress would bring her, I don't know, home. . . ." I feel my cheeks burn.

Missy looks lost. Then she gives me a hug. "I had no idea," she says. "I'm so sorry, Ky. I know this has to be really hard. Especially since you and your mom were always so close. I'll stop bugging you about the dress."

A few people clutching Chanel shopping bags walk by us

as we stand in silence for a few seconds. Missy does what she always does when she's confused: glosses her lips.

Then she pipes up. "Okay, so this is definitely not the right time to tell you this. But you know how before you were just joking about how I always knew who I'd be going to prom with . . . ?" She grows quiet.

"Yeah, and you didn't say anything. . . ."

"Well, you were right."

My heart stops in my chest.

"Don't be mad, but this morning, Andrew surprised me at my front door. . . ." She trails off.

"And?" I slow my pace.

"And I looked like total trash, but uh, that's besides the point. . . ." She pauses again.

"And!" I fake shout, turning to face her. My stomach flips. *Please say you said no. Please say you said no.*

She sighs. "And when I opened the door, all I saw was a ton of yellow roses. Like a million. Anyway, there was Andrew and he handed me the roses and there was a tiny note attached to the bunch. It said, 'Roses are yellow. Violets are blue. Will you make my prom dreams come true?'" Missy pauses, looking at me for a response.

"What about your whole revenge plan?" I ask, confused about how things could have taken such a drastic turn.

"Forget about revenge. Isn't that romantic?!?" she squeals.

For a second, I don't say anything. Then I squeeze Missy's hand, collecting myself before I throw up. "That's great, Miss."

"I know. I'm so psyched. . . . Now I really have a reason to get a Banana Fad dress of my own! Isn't this exciting!"

Yeah, exciting.

Missy detects that I'm not entirely happy for her. "I'm sorry. It must be tough to hear this with the whole Zach thing."

The Zach thing? "So, let me get this straight. All is forgiven with Andrew even though he was a cheater too. But not with Zachary?" I place my hand on my hip.

Missy's eyes widen. "But Andrew didn't win the contest."

Gotta love the logic.

twenty-two

"There's our softball stud!" Brooke Lauder calls out as I make my way into the school quad for the junior class assembly. I eye Brooke suspiciously. Besides Missy, she's my only other real threat for prom princess. (Unless Missy is wrong and losing Zachary and my softball spot have totally spoiled my chances.)

"Come sit down!" Missy exclaims. Missy and Brooke are spread out on the kelly green grass, devouring a plate of strawberries, mangoes, and red grapes. Andrew, Nick, and Brett sit beside them.

I fall down onto the grass and take it all in. The lawn feels like a soft comfy carpet. Across from me is a huge, white gazebo with an enormous dessert table. Next to the gazebo is a small stage decorated with balloons and a BEACHWOOD ACADEMY PROM COURT banner. Everything is royal blue and white, our school colors. Round tables dot the courtyard.

"Ky! How's it going?" Phoenix stops in front of me, blocking my view. "Are you nervous?"

Is she asking if I'm nervous because she thinks I'm not going to be selected?

"What?" I snap.

Phoenix. I didn't even think of Phoenix as a potential problem. Pheonix was on the Snow Ball Court in eighth grade. She'll definitely make it.

"Prom court. You're a shoo-in," Phoenix says.

"Oh. Yeah," I say, deflating like a balloon.

"I still can't believe prom and the Desert Invitational are on the same day. What a bummer." Phoenix sighs.

"Yeah, sucks big time," Eva adds, joining us.

I'm tempted to say: *No, living in your boyfriend's backyard with no mom who understands you sucks big time.* But instead I keep it simple. "Uh-huh . . ."

They give each other a look that says, *Let's get out of here. Kylie's gonna blow.* Then, in a rush, they say, "See ya!" and bolt.

"Aren't the strawberries divine?" Brooke says, totally clueless about what just happened. She crosses her outstretched legs, bringing together the thigh-high socks she wore to go with her miniskirt.

"You're so European now. You even have the faux Madonna accent. . . ." Missy snickers, popping a piece of melon into her mouth.

Nick butts in. "So, I hear there are only three spots for girls on prom court."

"So?" Brooke says, annoyed that anyone would get in the way of her strawberry-popping session.

"So, there's three of you here. And like two hundred other

junior girls." Nicks grabs a strawberry straight out of Brooke's hand and scarfs it down.

"You pig!" Brooke pouts.

"I try. But really, are you girls going to pull each other's hair out?"

Missy eyes them conspiratorially. "We aren't going to have to. We're the only ones who matter."

Brett and Andrew crack up at that one. Nick shakes his head and says, "Keep dreaming." Then he gets up and walks over to the spread. Andrew immediately follows suit. A second later, Brett glances at me and does the same.

As the guys walk away, I think to myself: *Nick's right. There's only room for three girls on the court. Brooke and Missy will make it. And then, Phoenix will be called too. And I'll be left out. The class won't vote for a benchwarmer.*

A familiar voice interrupts my disastrous train of thought. "How's our future princess?" Zachary asks. He sits down next to me, places two plates to his left, and begins running his fingers through my blonde locks. "I know of at least one worthy prince," he whispers.

My cheeks heat up. I glance at Missy and see that she's staring at us. "Whatever," I say, quickly scooching away from Zachary.

But not before Missy decides that she wants to put some distance between herself and the Murph Man.

"Uh, Ky," Missy says. "I think Brooke and I are going to go see how Ms. Sealer is handling all the preparations."

"Yeah, for the announcement *très important*," Brooke says.

Then they both get up.

When I turn back to Zachary, he's holding two plates filled with treats. "Sweets for my girl," he announces. He hands me a plate with a chocolate chip cookie, two strawberries, and a cherry-cheese Danish.

"Nice line, Romeo." I roll my eyes. From a distance, I swear I can hear Missy and Brooke gossiping about me. I stand up.

"Where are you going?" Zachary asks.

"Uh, to hit up the buffet."

"But what about the plate I got you?"

I calm the flutters in my stomach and remind myself that I'm in front of my friends. "I'm quite capable of getting my own, thank you."

Then I turn around and bump into my worst nightmare. Amber.

"Hey, Ky!" She beams, looking more pink than pale.

What's going on? She's supposed to be dying! (Or something.)

"Isn't this delish? We never had this kind of spread at my old school. Our junior prom was like no big deal. Here it's absolutely huge! I'm so excited to . . ." A donut rolls off her plate and plops on the grass. "Oops." She giggles.

I stare at it. Then I look up at her. "Wait. What the heck are you doing here?"

Amber's freckled-covered nose wrinkles. "What are you talking about? I go here, remember?" She giggles again, in her cute, *you-can't-hate-me* voice.

"No. I mean, what are you doing back? I thought you were sick!" I kind of scream the last word.

"Oh. Yeah, that." She gets a better hold on her plate of fruit and Danish. "I'm all better now. Just needed forty-eight hours of antibiotics. I get strep all the time. . . ."

I try to think fast. "Then you should really get your tonsils out soon. Like don't even wait for softball season to be over. They could get really bad."

"Oh, don't worry!" Amber giggles some more. "There's nothing wrong with my tonsils. By the way . . ." Her face lights up. "Thanks so much for filling in for me yesterday."

Filling in? Urgh!! She took my spot.

"I heard you did amazing. We're really a great team!"

When were we ever a team?

"I almost forgot." She digs into the pocket of her jeans. "I made you this." Amber holds out a blue-and-white beaded necklace. "I'm so sorry about the starting spot. Hopefully this will brighten your day."

"Yeah . . . Thanks," I say, rolling my eyes as I grab the necklace. I shove it in my pocket and steady my nerves by feeling for the pendant around my neck.

"I just love B-Dub." Amber looks around at our classmates. Then her eyes flit to the stage. She covers her mouth with a napkin and moves in closer to my ear. "I wouldn't tell anyone else this, but since we're practice partners and all . . ."

Yeah, practice partners. Lucky me.

"I would totally die right here if I was picked to be on

the prom court. Not that I'd ever make it in a million years." She giggles for the umpteenth time.

No kidding you'd never make it.

Amber must not notice the irritated expression on my face because she continues. "But, it's weird. It's like this year, here at B-Dub, I feel like I'm coming into my own. Did you see how the lacrosse guys held up those *K* signs for me? Because of my strikeouts?"

"Yeah, I saw the signs all right." I snarl. *She's not the only one who got signs. . . .*

She sighs dramatically. "But I don't feel like a real B-Dub student yet. You know? And it's like if I made prom court, I would finally prove to everyone that I'm a true Wildcat, and not just some girl who dropped in out of nowhere because her parents got divorced." She pauses. "Do you know what I mean?"

Yeah, actually, I do. But honestly, what does she want me to say? First she swipes my spot. Now she wants prom court? If she thinks I'm letting her take that too . . .

"Okay, students, take your seats," Ms. Sealer shouts into the microphone. "It's time to announce the court."

"Amber!" Danielle yells out from one of the picnic tables.

"See ya." Amber beams at me. Swiftly, she jogs over to Danielle, waving at me as she goes.

"Yeah, good luck. You're gonna need it," I say, with every ounce of sarcasm I possess. Fortunately, she's too far away to catch my tone.

I make my way to the picnic table where Missy is sitting with some of our other friends. As I settle into a fabric-covered chair, I take a deep breath. *This is my moment*, I think. *I'm not going to let Amber get to me.*

I reach over to Missy's plate to grab a grape when I catch sight of the table next to us. It's filled with the usual suspects—Zachary, Nick, Andrew, Brett, Dwight, and the rest of the guys from the basketball team. As always, they're goofing off. All of that would be fine except that Zachary isn't participating. In fact, he isn't even looking at them.

He's looking directly at Amber.

twenty-three

"It's that time of year again!" Ms. Sealer, our student council club advisor, shouts.

The courtyard fills with cheers.

"Give it to me, cougar," Nick yells.

Missy makes a big show of rolling her eyes at Nick. Then she whispers to me, "Sealer and Chris Olay were so last year."

A few administrators charge toward Nick.

He shrugs like he knew this was only a matter of time, and follows the staff out of the quad.

Ms. Sealer clears her throat and smoothes out the wrinkles in her Tahari suit. "Time to announce the junior class prom court! Remember, your prom prince and princess will be chosen from this court."

This is it. . . .

Again, cheers erupt, this time even louder than the last.

Missy eyes me, meaningfully—I can't tell if it's meant to be the look of a competitor or a friend.

"Just a reminder that the prom will be held at the Beachwood Country Club two weeks from Saturday." Ms. Sealer tensely clicks her Jimmy Choo heel against the edge of the microphone base. (All this work must be getting to her.)

Then she continues. "We will have a royal-blue carpet at the club entrance. And we will be . . ."

I begin to lose focus on what Ms. Sealer is saying and take stock of the girls sitting around my table—Missy, Brooke, Phoenix. *How many of them are actually threats?*

I feel myself starting to get queasy and force myself to pay attention.

"As you know, we traditionally do things a little bit differently here at Beachwood." Ms. Sealer pauses, pulling out a crinkled piece of paper from her jacket pocket. "You voted three junior girls and boys to represent you on the junior class court. From this selection, one girl and one boy will be chosen as your prince and princess come prom night." She claps her hands, further crinkling the paper between her palms.

A few classmates clap, looking around nervously.

"First off, I'm going to name the girls," she says, looking as if this is some kind of great revelation.

"Ladies first!" Andrew yells out.

Then silence fills the air.

Please call my name. Please call my name.

"Missy Adams."

Missy lets out a little cheer and jumps out of her chair, nearly knocking it over. She makes a beeline for the stage and beams as Ms. Sealer places the royal-blue sash over her black Theory tank.

My stomach lurches.

Missy gives me a tiny wave as a hush falls over the audience once again.

Please call my name. Please call my name.

"Brooke Lauder."

More woots and cheers.

Brooke delicately stands up and sashays up to the stage. Ms. Sealer lays the sash on top of her Rebecca Taylor cardigan.

This is it . . . my last shot.

My stomach literally sloshes back and forth.

"And finally, I'm proud to announce . . ."

Don't let it be Phoenix.

"Kylie Collins."

For a second, I don't move.

More cheers ring out. I hear Amber whistle as I gingerly make my way toward the stage. I stand next to Missy and she squeezes my hand. "We did it," she whispers as Ms. Sealer lays the sash over my shoulder.

I look up at the hundreds of students staring at us. Eva claps wildly. Phoenix manages to pull herself out of her obvious disappointment to whistle. Brett screams, "Yeah, Ky-lie!" I breathe relief. *At least something in my life went right.* I can't wait to tell my mom.

"Now for the guys," Ms. Sealer announces.

I'm so on cloud nine that I don't care what people

think—I try to sneak a peek at the one guy I really care about. Even if his eyes weren't where they were supposed to be just moments ago. But that's when I realize that he's not at his table.

Before I know what I'm doing, I find myself searching for Amber. Finally, I find her at a table with Danielle and a bunch of random girls who I barely know. And who should be sitting next to her but Zachary Michael Murphy.

What the . . . If he's trying to grab some fresh meat, I'm gonna . . .

I try to divert my eyes. Maybe Zachary's just trying to dig up some info on Amber's transfer.

But I can't manage to convince myself that that's really what he's up to. I look back at them. By now, Amber's leaning against Zachary's toned right arm.

My breath catches in my throat as the prom court announcements continue.

"Andrew Mason."

Here we go.

Andrew steps up onstage and plants a sweet kiss on Missy's cheek. He tosses his sash over his head and files behind her, beginning the second horizontal line.

I start breathing faster. Zachary is a shoo-in. He better look away from Amber soon or he's going to miss his name. Not to mention other things in his life . . . like me.

"Matt Moore."

Taylor's boyfriend. Any other day and I'd be pissed that

Taylor even came close to being a part of all this. But not today. Today I'm too busy trying to figure out why *my* Zachary is talking to *my* arch nemesis.

Matt looks around sheepishly and moves behind Brooke. Ms. Sealer awkwardly attempts to place the sash across his hoodie. After a while, she gives up and hands the sash to Matt. He shoves it in his front pocket.

"And last but certainly not least, Zachary Murphy."

Zachary skips the steps, hops onto the stage, and grabs his sash from Sealer. He confidently walks right up to me.

Oh no you don't.

He tries to hug me, but I step to the side. Then he lunges toward me again, attempting to plant a kiss on my cheek. I move like I'm in the batter's box avoiding brushback pitches.

"Congratulations to all the nominees," Ms. Sealer shouts, ignoring the face-off between me and Zachary. Turning to the crowd, she announces, "This is your Beachwood Academy Junior Prom Court." Then she waves for us to move together for a picture.

Immediately, everyone begins to wrap their arms around one another. Still avoiding Zachary, I sprint to the other side of the pack. Then I shove between Brooke and Matt Moore, secretly enjoying the fact that Zachary's attention is back to where it should be. Me.

Zachary follows, annoying the prom court's other members. He maneuvers between Matt Moore and me, wrapping his arm around my shoulders. I'm too squished in to move.

"Congrats, Ky," he says in my ear.

Tingles creep down my spine.

"See, me and you. It's fate. Now you gotta to go to the prom with me."

I turn around to wrestle Zachary's arm off my shoulders. I haven't had time to sort out the zillion emotions still swirling in my stomach. I don't want our fates to be sealed together for all photographic eternity.

Of course, that's when Zachary kisses my cheek.

And before I have a chance to wiggle away, my fate is decided for me: Ms. Sealer snaps the photo.

twenty-four

"Welcome to Baja Spa and Salon," a woman in all black announces as the girls from the basketball team and I make our way into the spa the night after the pre-prom assembly.

Before we even have a chance to take in our surroundings, a man steps between Missy and me. "Hors d'oeuvre?" he asks. He holds out a shiny silver plate filled with olives, cheese spread, crackers, and fruit. Like the receptionist, he's also dressed in all black. (Must be the uniform here . . .)

Missy and I both grab napkins. She snatches up some black olives, while I grab crackers, cheese spread, and strawberries. We giggle when our fingers bump.

"Savage." Missy laughs.

"You know I can't say no to cheese spread," I say.

I'm about to ask the other girls—Eva, Tamika, Taylor, Jessica—if they're enjoying their own selections from the hors d'oeuvre tray when a woman with straight blonde hair comes over to us. She has that *I'm-too-cool-to-be-here* look that screams "stylist." Like her fellow Baja Salon employees, she's sporting an impressive all-black ensemble, although in her case she's livened things up with a chunky gold necklace and heeled ankle boots.

Sure enough, the blonde woman announces, "I'm Avery. I'll be one of your stylists today."

I scarf down my last remaining cracker as she continues.

"Why don't you girls follow me and the other stylists and I"—she motions to five similarly attired women—"will begin your hair consultations."

We trail Avery down a long, gold-painted hallway to the styling stations, and she continues to explain the course of today's events. "I'm told that some of you will be sampling hairstyles for prom. Is that correct?"

"Absolutely!" Jessica exclaims.

Tamika quickly steps in to correct her. "They are. My senior prom isn't for another few weeks. I'm just here for extensions."

Missy looks like she's about to inform Avery that a few of Baja's stylists will actually be coming to her house the night of the prom when Avery turns around abruptly and catches sight of Tamika. "Oh, you must be Tamika!" she says. "You're the spitting image of your mother. She told me to expect you today. She's one of our favorite clients!"

Tamika shuffles around uncomfortably. Avery, satisfied that she's made nice with one of her "favorite clients'" daughters, motions to each of our seats. I'm surprised when, for all Avery's talk of Tamika's mother, I'm the one assigned to her. Still, with all the stations located in a row, it's not like she's out of anyone's earshot. "And are any of you girls on prom court?" she asks, looking left and right.

"Uh? Hello?" Missy replies. "Only like all of us. Well, me, my best friend Kylie"—she leans over from her spot next to mine, giving me a nudge—"and our darling friend Tamika."

"Actually, I'm on the senior court," Tamika chimes in. "But for some reason I still hang out with these midgets."

Somehow Tamika's attitude just bounces off of Avery. "Ooooh. Very nice. What cut is your dress?" She asks, turning her attention to me as she finger-combs my hair.

Missy glances at me through the reflection of the adjacent mirror. Before she can say anything, her stylist, a bald man in his early thirties, summons her to the sinks.

"I don't exactly have a dress yet," I say. I look down and begin to pick at the silk black cover-up. "Or a date," I squeak.

"Well, a girl as gorgeous as you are can wear any dress she wants. So any hairstyle, up or down, will work with your beautiful mane. It's just a matter of what you like best." She smiles at me through the mirror. "And believe me, you'll get a date. I'm sure the guys at your school are lining up to take you to the prom."

"That's what I've been telling her!" Jessica calls out, whipping around to face me. As she does, she disrupts her hair stylist, who's experimenting with a French twist.

Yeah, if by lining up, they mean Zachary and . . . Zachary.

"Okay, let's take you over to have your hair washed." Avery brings me over to a young stylist-in-training by the sinks.

The trainee wraps a black robe around me and sits me down, checking to see if the water temperature is okay.

Missy is already seated at the sink next to mine. With her head now wrapped in a white towel, she leans my way. "I'm overseeing some sketches Hannah is working on just in case you change your mind about the dress." She winks.

I shake my head, thinking to myself that it's good that Hannah isn't here to hear this.

Then I catch sight of Eva walking back to her stylist's station. A towel is draped around her neck, but it doesn't hide her white earbuds. I decide to shift the focus away from me. "Eva!" I call out. "Are you actually listening to music while you're getting your hair done?"

Eva doesn't respond. She just taps her foot to her own private concert as she settles back into her chair.

"Eva!" I yell again.

Finally, Eva pulls one of the buds from her ear, visibly annoying her hairstylist. "Sorry, I can't hear anything. I'm too busy checking out tracks for Xavier's big gigs." She places the earbud back in her ear.

"Where is he playing?" Taylor asks. She unwraps her long legs out from under her.

Eva must hear *that* because she manages to respond on the first go-round. "Oh, you know. Vi's annual spring fling. And . . . prom!"

"Oh my gosh! That's amazing!" Jessica shrieks. Her stylist now looks as annoyed as Eva's.

"What else would you expect from 'DJ Buzz Cut Cali'?" Eva asks, twirling an earbud in one hand.

"So, who's going to Vi's party on Saturday?" Taylor asks. Compared to the rest of us, she's hardly moved around at all since we sat down, so her updo is actually starting to take shape.

"Wouldn't miss it," Missy says, grabbing a red grape off a leftover silver tray. "You're going, right, Ky?"

"Of course I am." I eye Missy suspiciously. "Why wouldn't I? Vi throws the best parties of the year."

"Yeah, remember the Halloween Hayride?" Missy asks, reminding me of Vi's last big bash.

A cute brunette assistant applies keratin to Missy's wet hair.

Missy doesn't let up. "Remember when you caught Zachary on a one-on-one hayride with Chloe?" she asks.

Okay, I get it. Missy thinks he's a jerk because he won the stupid list. But why does she have to constantly remind me?

"And that was before the rumors flew about Zachary and Chloe over Christmas break. Do you remember?" Missy looks at me.

Do I . . . I begin to pick at the lining of my cover-up again, if only to stop myself from reminding Missy that today was a dumb day to get her hair straightened—she's going to still be here long after the rest of us are gone.

"Who could forget when tool-man Nick dressed up like

Violet?" Tamika adds. "He was all decked out in Vi's homecoming dress from last year. That was hilarious."

"I know! I think I'm scarred for life. I don't know who was showing more boob that night, Nick or Chloe Simpson." Missy glances at me.

How can Missy keep doing this? I glare at her. *Why would she purposely mention Chloe twice? Is she trying to remind me of Zachary's mistakes? Or is she just trying to embarrass me?*

"We're all dying to know: are you going with Zach?" Tamika turns toward me. "You've been so busy with softball, I haven't had the chance to ask you."

"Keep your head straight, please," Tamika's stylist firmly states, while beginning to pin back sections of her hair.

"Is Chloe Simpson entering a convent?" I sneer.

"Uh, no . . ." Taylor says, clearly confused.

"Good. Because she's as likely to do that as I'll be to go to the prom with Zachary," I say, looking back at my buds to make sure they buy what I'm selling.

My basketball buds giggle. Even Taylor grins.

We're all caught off guard when the people doing our hair interject. "I so miss high school." Avery sighs.

"Not me," Eva's stylist replies. She begins to brush out Eva's hair.

I decide to dig for more dirt. "You going with Dwight?" I ask Tamika.

"We're going as friends this year. With graduation and

college coming up, I can't handle the whole relationship thing right now." Tamika pulls a magazine out of the rack by her feet.

"Friends with bennies." Eva looks up from her iPod.

"How did Matt pop the prom question to you, Taylor?" Missy asks as her stylist rolls her blonde hair in oversized curlers.

I feel for my heart charm. *I could have Zachary if I wanted him. All I have to do is say the word. . . .*

Taylor lowers the glass she's sipping from and places it on a nearby table. She hesitates for a second and looks at Missy. Finally, she spouts, "It was amazing. . . . Matt took me to the beach two weeks ago. The same spot we went to when we first met up one night after a game at the beach courts."

Grr . . . Of course little miss Taylor didn't mention what else she did on the beach courts (aka hook up with a certain Zachary Murphy—a Zachary Murphy that belonged and still belongs to *me*).

A few seconds later, Taylor's voice pulls me out of my head. "Matt had a whole picnic set up for me with all my favorite foods. When I opened the basket, a note was inside."

"Awwww . . ." Tamika, Eva, and Missy sing.

"That's so sweet," Avery adds.

I stare at my stylist as she experiments by twisting my hair tight against my head.

"Let me guess, the note said, 'Will you go to the prom with me?'" Missy yells over the sound of a blow dryer.

Taylor shakes her head. "Better. It was a clue that led to another clue, to another, and then to a spot with a bunch of seashells." She smiles. "When I looked closer, I realized he spelled out—"

Missy finishes her sentence. "Will you go to the prom with me?"

Taylor corrects her. "Yeah, but in seashells."

"Aww . . ." rings out through the spa again.

For God's sake. Please give me a brush so I can jam the handle down my throat.

"How did Xavier ask you, Eva? At some club?" Jessica asks.

Eva rests her leg over the side of the chair and pops out her earbuds. "You know it! Saturday night. He announced it DJ style." She pretends to scratch some records while sticking out her tongue to the side.

The group bursts out in giggles as she mocks her boyfriend.

I don't. Not because it's not funny. Eva's hilarious. Because everyone in this salon has lost their mind.

"He totally sticks out his tongue like that when he's working." Tamika cracks up.

I guess Missy feels like we're veering too far away from talking about her because she pipes up. "So, are you guys ready to wear your Banana Fad dresses?"

"Where is our resident designer?" I ask.

"Hannah's working hard on the dresses," Taylor says. "She's swamped."

Of course.

"Is everyone wearing Hannah's designs?" I look around at the girls.

"Yup," they answer in unison.

"They're originals. Who wouldn't?" Tamika shrugs.

"What's Banana Fad?" Avery asks, obviously eager to be the first to get in on all the latest trends.

"Oh, it's only the hottest new name in fashion," Missy declares.

No, it's not. I can't let that one slide. "It's a thing Missy's doing with another girl in our high school."

Missy looks horrified. "A thing?" she asks.

"Ideally, it's Missy's ticket into college," I explain.

"Really?" Avery asks.

"Well, if by 'ticket,' Kylie means that admissions officers are going to love the marketing portfolio I develop through this enterprise, then yeah," Missy clarifies, taking a sip of her water.

"Oh . . ." The stylists look at each other and smile.

"Are all of you girls wearing these dresses?" Missy's stylist asks.

"The bigger question is: Is *Kylie* wearing Banana Fad?" Tamika eyes me.

I point to the ceiling again. "Are pigs flying?" I look at Missy and grin. "Just kidding."

Missy's smile disappears and she takes another gulp of her water.

"Relax, Miss. It's not like I'm saying anything bad about *you*. I mean, it's not your so-called enterprise."

Missy drowns her frustrations in her water.

"And the best part about wearing Banana Fad is none of us had to register our dresses online on that insane Beachwood prom page because each one is an original," Taylor says, ignoring my comment.

"So true," Missy adds. She shoots me a snotty look.

"What, Missy hire you to spout off commercials for Banana Fad?" I toss a strawberry at Taylor, who catches it.

"Nice catch," Missy says. "Maybe Taylor should try out for softball." She looks at me. "Maybe *she* can pitch." Missy smirks.

What a bit—

"B-ball only for me," she says, stretching out her long thin legs across the gleaming floor. "My hands are for inside the paint." Taylor holds up her massive man hands.

"I know. I wish Hannah was here to hear this, but I'm seriously impressed with her. I mean, you should see the dresses," Missy says. "She's good for a little girl."

"I'm impressed with her and I don't even know her," Missy's stylist adds, smoothing out Missy's platinum hair.

"Hannah's the bomb." Taylor giggles.

Hannah's not the bomb. Not this day, this month, this year.

"Missy, you never told us how Andrew asked you," Jessica says.

Oh please, not another invite story. I feel myself start to

hyperventilate and tear off the silk cover-up. I climb off the chair—there's no way I'm hearing about Andrew and his roses one more time. "Excuse me," I say to Avery. "I have to go."

"But we're not done here," Avery implores.

"I'll be right back."

I run back through the hallway, ignoring the chorus of "Ky!" and "Where is she going?" Then I step through the glass doors. I just need some air.

I take deep breaths and pull my phone out of my pocket, attempting to distract myself. That's when I notice the red light is blinking. Quickly, I tap on my voice mail.

"Hey, Ky. You want romance?" says Zachary's recorded voice. "I've got me some romance." He clears his throat. "Roses are red. Violets are blue. I need a prom date. How about you?"

I hit "delete." Next message.

"Hey, Kylie. It's Amber. I was wondering if you could, er, um, include me in your limo for prom? If not, I understand. Bye. Oh. And my number is—"

Once again, I hit "delete." And for the last one . . .

"Hi, sweetie, it's Mom. I just wanted to thank you for leaving me a message about your prom court nomination. I'm so proud of you, honey."

Chills sprint up my back.

"I'm going to fly in on Friday so we can go shopping. Text me when you get a chance and let me know who you're going with this year. I'm assuming it's Mr. Zachary Michael Murphy. See you soon."

I save Mom's message.

Finally.

My breathing's returned to normal, so I turn around to rejoin my buds inside the salon. As I pull open the glass doors, I'm assaulted with another prom invite story. I freeze when I hear Tamika rambling something about Hershey's Kisses and Dwight saying he "kisses the ground Tamika walks on."

I let go of the door and turn back to the outside world. Again, I pull out my phone. And without looking at it, my fingers know what to do.

Zachary answers on the first ring.

twenty-five

The next day at an away game, I'm planted on the bench once again, feeling sorry for myself. I should be psyched—Coach announced we earned our spot in the prestigious Desert Invitational tournament for the first time in ten years. Plus, we're playing Richland, our biggest basketball rivals, who we just beat in the championship game a few short months ago. But I'm not. Because I won't really be a part of it. At this point, I'm just a spectator.

I try to calm myself by thinking about what a nice convo I had with Zachary last night. As usual, he knew how to talk me off the ledge, so much so that after we spoke, I was relaxed enough to finish up my salon appointment and make small talk with the other girls.

When I see my teammates begin to run in from the field, I scoot across the bench, farther away from Chloe and Sophia and closer to Emily. At least, she's only benchwarming because of an injury.

I wave at Zoe as she comes into the dugout, having just finished up another inning catching for the ever-amazing Amber. (Who, to add salt to the wound, is on her way to pitching a perfect game.) "Here." I point to the spot I just vacated. "I kept it nice and warm for you."

"You'll be back out there in no time," Zoe says, plopping down between Emily and me. She drops her catcher's mask on the bench between us. "And anyway, rest up because we'll need you next week for the Desert Invitational. I can't wait!"

"Yeah. Sure. I'll keep telling myself that. . . ." The sounds of the other girls chatting and giggling starts to distract me. Emily has even been drawn into conversation with Sophia.

Zoe puts her hand on my shoulder, pulling me back in. "No, seriously, Ky. We've all said it before: the only question is how you're going to get all prettied up for prom in time."

"Zoe, I appreciate that you're trying to cheer me up and everything, but honestly, I'd probably be fine showing up to the tournament in full hair and makeup. It's not like I'm going to have a chance to get dirty."

I watch as Amber shuffles back onto the softball diamond. Like a kid on a playground, she's all giddy. When she sees me, she grins and waves. "Hey, pitching partner!"

I attempt to smile back, but I'm pretty sure my face just looks like a contorted grimace.

Zoe smacks my knee. "Will you stop it? You know you'll pitch at the Desert Invitational. . . . I mean, we can't play all our games on one arm. And you know Coach isn't going to put Sophia on the mound."

"Uh-huh . . ." I say. "Don't you need to go back out on the field?"

"Fine," Zoe says. "But this conversation isn't over." She jumps up from her seat and motions that she'll be watching me as she makes her way back to the field.

Now that the majority of the girls have left to go play their positions, Sophia takes this as an opportunity for us to catch up. "Can you believe Amber's throwing a perfect game?" She adjusts her messy ponytail.

I'm tempted not to respond, but I decide the better of it. "I know," I say, raising my voice in the hopes that someone will hear me. "But we're only through five innings."

"Still," Sophia says.

Emily leans over, her wrist still wrapped in a bandage. "Guys, shhh . . . or you'll ruin Amber's chances."

"You don't actually believe that silly superstition, do you?" Chloe asks, sliding over to talk to us.

"Who doesn't?" Emily says, disbelieving. No one wants to be responsible for jinxing a perfect game. One mention might be the end of it.

Not that I would know. I mean, it's not like I've ever thrown one.

Emily continues. "Did you see the guy in the stands with the UCLA polo sitting in front of Zoe's mom?" She points to the crowd with her uninjured hand.

"Anyone can have a UCLA polo," I reply. I scan the stands and spot the guy they're talking about.

"But he's not just anybody. He's a recruiter. And the woman next to him is from the University of Arizona. I remember them from last year." Emily pauses, picking a discarded batting glove up off the ground.

"They must have a break in their schedule today." Chloe winks. "Looks like they're here scouting."

"For real?" Sophia's eyes widen. "Who do you think they're here for?"

"Amber. Obviously," Chloe answers.

The more time I spend with Chloe, the less I like her.

"You okay, Ky?" Emily asks. "You look, I don't know. Kind of red."

"I'm fine," I say, feeling my face flush. I look out at the field and am met with an unwanted image: Amber and Danielle holding hands and jumping up and down after another hitless, scoreless inning.

They run, no, skip, back into the dugout. Clearly, they also saw the recruiters because the first thing I hear is Amber say, "Can you imagine? Me at UCLA?"

No . . . not her. Me.

"I can already picture you as a Bruin," Danielle replies, giving Amber a hug.

They squeal some more and resume jumping up and down.

And I can't help it: I bite my bottom lip until I taste blood.

twenty-six

"Safe!" the umpire shouts.

I jump up out of my seat. *Yes!* One of Richland's batters just made it to first base. Amber's chances of a perfect game are officially destroyed.

"Well, I guess we can't add Amber to the B-Dub history books," I think. Only my thought accidentally comes tumbling out of my mouth.

Chloe glances at me and sneers. "Don't sound so happy about it."

"I'm not. That sucks," I say, shrugging.

But *obviously* I am. Having to stare at Amber's perfect-game ball in the school trophy case for all eternity would have been just too much to bear.

Still, Amber manages to strike out the next batter.

I start to worry that people are going to forget that she *did* make a mistake when Coach Kate calls us in from the field. Then, to my surprise, she yells, "Kylie, grab your glove!"

I bounce up off the bench, do a calf stretch, and join my teammates outside the dugout. *Finally*, I'm going in.

But my excitement is short-lived.

Murmurs of "Did you see that?" and "Amazing" taunt me as I make my way toward Coach. *Ugh* . . . I can't believe that even now, when it's *my* turn, people are still talking about *her*.

I wait for Coach's instructions. When she's finished going over the lineup with Coach Jackie, she looks at me. "We're up by five. You're going in next inning. Go warm up with Emily," she says.

A little swirl settles in my stomach. I jog toward the pitching cage and wait for Emily as she quickly suits up in the dugout. Even though her wrist isn't yet strong enough to play on, it *has* healed enough for her to help out with practicing.

"There she is . . . the Beachwood Academy fallen star," an annoying squeaky voice announces behind me.

When I turn around, I spot Rob Hamilton, a reporter from the school newspaper, the *Sand Dollar*. He stares at me from the other side of the pitching cage fence. In one hand he holds a silver voice recorder. I visibly shudder. Rob says that "the newspaper is the most powerful club in the school." I just think he's a tabloid journalist, a weasel who starts fires, then walks away.

He holds the recorder up to his mouth. "I'm here with Kylie Collins, the Beachwood Academy pitcher best known for her junk pitches. Collins, how does it feel to be demoted to second string?"

Is he for real? He's going to do this right now? Right before I take the mound?

He holds his recorder over the fence, urging me to give him a statement.

Hello? Does he realize that he's not exactly a broadcast journalist?

I refuse to fall into his trap. Quickly, I turn my back toward him, balance my glove between my knees, and adjust the ribbons wrapped around my ponytail.

But Rob doesn't take no for an answer. "What are your thoughts on Amber McDonald, the Southern California powerhouse who transferred here this spring?"

"No comment," I say, still facing away from him.

"Really? You don't have anything to say about that rise ball of hers or the perfect game that she nearly pitched?" He continues to prod.

I stay silent.

"Does it hurt?" Rob asks, tucking his yellow pencil behind his ear. "It must. But I guess we all knew this was coming. . . ."

That's it. I drop my glove and take a step toward Rob, eager to show him what a "second string" can do to his face. As I'm about to grab his recorder (and hopefully his neck), Coach Kate yells, "Kylie, you're in."

I shake Rob off. I'm not going to let him rain on my parade. Then I bend down, grab my glove, and am about to set up on the mound when I hear Rob say, "Don't look so confident. You're only going in now because you guys are up by five thanks to Amber."

"Rob, just get out of my way," I reply.

And that's when he says the worst thing of all: "Even you can't mess this up."

twenty-seven

"Please open up to yesterday's homework," Mrs. Cunningham announces.

I'm sitting on a hard chair, staring at the clock. How can I think about pre-calc when my mom is currently on her way here? To the West Coast! Sure, my performance on the mound yesterday wasn't exactly top-notch. (I gave up three hits and one run.) But finally, I'm going to go prom shopping! And with no time left to spare, too, since prom is a little over a week away. Now I just have to figure out who I'm going to go with.

"Let's divide up into groups to go over the problems," Mrs. Cunningham continues.

As I move my desk over to Missy, I see that Hannah is already there. I can't get over what a strange pair she and Hannah make. Where Hannah's arms are covered with weird metal bracelets that look like they were fashioned out of loose wires, Missy has a single David Yurman birthstone cable bracelet wrapped around her wrist. In what twisted universe would two people who are so different be partners? They're polar opposites.

"Okay, what are we doing? I missed the problem," I say, plopping on the chair.

"I'm not feeling the lace right here." Hannah points her pencil eraser at the top of a prom dress design, ignoring me. "I think it's going to clash with—"

"Hello, what problem?" I ask, louder this time.

"One sec . . ." Missy says.

"Let me see." I snatch up the sketchbook and stare at a sketch of an electric-blue silk dress with black lace above the knees. It's reminiscent of Madonna's *Like a Virgin* vintage piece from the eighties. And strangely enough, I actually like it.

I'm about to say as much to Hannah when I spot Martie looking at me from the doorway. Mrs. Cunningham walks over to meet her.

"Kylie!" Nick catcalls from across the room.

"What, loser?" I roll my eyes.

"I heard that you got lucky yesterday. . . ."

Immediately, my thoughts turn to Zachary. "What are you talking about?" I ask.

Nick smirks. "Heard you actually played in the game against Richland." Nick strolls over and straddles a chair in front of me. "How'd that happen?"

"Heard you don't have a date for the prom. I definitely know how that happened." I tilt my head. Before I turn my attention back to pre-calc, I glance at Brett Davidson in the back of the room. He diverts his eyes like he's been doing ever since that day when our convo was interrupted.

Missy, Hannah, and Phoenix giggle behind me.

"I have a date. . . ." Nick cocks his chin and puffs out his chest like a rooster.

"Oh yeah. Who?" I ask.

"January Lemmons," he says.

"Another freshman." I roll my eyes. "Too bad I didn't get to tell her how much of a jerk you are."

A few more classmates giggle.

"Whatever . . ." Nick stands up and returns to his seat.

I use this opportunity to meander back toward Brett. "Hey," I say, waiting for him to make his move. When he doesn't, I do it for him. "Is there something you wanted to ask me?"

He looks up at me. "Uh. About that . . ." He pauses. "Yeah, but . . . I, uh, asked someone else."

So, he was going to ask me to prom. I take a deep breath and give him an answer that no one would expect from me. "No worries."

Brett looks at me to see if I'm joking. "What?"

"You just made another decision I had to make a whole lot easier."

deep brown eyes stare intently into mine. "What I want to know is, do you still love the game of softball?"

"Of course I do."

"Then remember what I said: that's all that matters."

I glance at the clock. Mom's plane landed at LAX an hour ago.

"I want to reiterate what I said last time we spoke: I heard you're quite the second baseman for your ASA team."

"Yeah, I guess." I shrug.

Dress shopping . . . Dress shopping . . .

Martie smiles, looking satisfied. "Then here's the plan. Approach Coach Kate this weekend during practice and tell her that you want to start training to be a utility player. Continue to work hard on your pitching, hitting, and fielding. That way you'll be a more versatile player and a real asset to the team."

"But I'm a pitcher, not a second baseman." I place my books and my bag on the desk next to me.

"Yet." She grins.

"Look, Coach, I appreciate your help. Really, I do. And again, I'm sorry for the way I behaved. But I've got a lot on my mind right now."

"Just promise me you'll think about it." She gently smiles. "When the game changes, you have to change with it."

"Thanks . . ." I pick up my things and dart out of the classroom before Martie can get another word in.

Once I reach the hallway, I sprint toward my locker, spin

twenty-eight

Before I can make a beeline to my dress-shopping extravaganza, Mrs. Cunningham calls out to me. "Kylie, Martie would like to speak with you for a second."

"Hi, Kylie." Martie looks at me with concern.

What now?

"Hey, Coach," I say, still feeling bad about the way I treated her a few weeks ago after the roster posting.

Mrs. Cunningham gathers her books and leaves me and Martie alone together in the classroom.

"Got a sec?" she asks.

I adjust my bag.

"I saw your game the other day." Martie crosses her arms across her cotton polo. "You pitched well."

"Thanks," I say, assuming she must be talking about the game I pitched against Bel Air. But still, it's nice for her to talk to me at all after the way I acted. "Look, Coach, I'm sorry for—"

Martie cuts me off. "Don't worry about it. I know you were under a lot of stress. It's water under the bridge." Her the combo, and swing open the door. Then I shove my hand in my Under Armour bag.

I pull out my phone to let my mom know I'm running late, and see that the message indicator light is already blinking. I quickly touch the screen. Sure enough, there's a text from my mom.

FR: MOM

SORRY, SWEETS. HAD 2 STAY NYC 4 WKND 4 WRK. C U SOON.

My eyes fill with hot tears. *How could she do this?* I hurl the phone against a set of lockers across the hall. It ricochets off the metal, smacks the ground, and slides across the concrete floor. I lean my head and tap it against my locker.

She promised! Why can't she just give me one weekend? And how could she possibly think that a last-minute text is the right way to let me down?

I open the door wider and stare at my flaming red face in my locker mirror. I attempt to take slow, cleansing breaths, and let go, like I hear my dad yapping about during his nightly sessions. *I will not cry. She won't make me cry again.*

"Did you drop something?" I see Zachary's face appear next to mine in my mirror.

I look at him through the reflection, his eyes full of concern, and it hits me: *I didn't do this. She doesn't deserve my tears.*

twenty-nine

"Just come on!" Zachary yells a few hours later. He rides ahead of me on his beach cruiser, having convinced me to meet him after practice with talk of how I deserve to be treated better and a confession about his father's recent bender.

"Chill out. I'm right behind you." I attempt to keep up on the wooden beach path. After a tough late practice (during which I followed Martie's advice and took a few ground balls at second—to surprising success) and all the drama with my mom, I'm struggling tonight.

"Stop whining." He stands up on the pedals, expanding his upper body like a knight riding a chariot. A breeze rustles through his white Los Angeles Lakers tee and mesh shorts.

"Where are we going?" I ask, pumping the pedals harder to keep up.

"You'll see . . ." Zachary makes a right off the path and onto the street. I follow him without questioning. Then, all of a sudden, it hits me.

"Wait. Are we going to our old elementary school?" In the distance, the familiar building looms. The Spanish-style architecture is the same, but the school itself used to seem much bigger and scarier.

"Just wait and see. . . ." Zachary veers off into the bus parking lot and bikes around the building toward the back. Once he reaches the fence that lines the playground, he dismounts his bike and leans it against the fence. He walks up to me and holds out his hand in an attempt to help me off my bike.

"What do you think, I can't do it myself?" I say, jumping off and kicking out my kickstand.

He grins. "See, you don't let me be romantic. And you complain about the way I invited you to prom . . ."

"Yeah, I do. But that's not the point. Helping me off a bike I'm completely capable of dismounting myself isn't romantic. It's male chauvinism at its best."

"Did somebody forget to drink her Caramel Frap this morning?" Zachary teases me, pulling me toward the playground. At first I resist, but then I follow him. He sits on the end of a purple-and-blue enclosed plastic slide. Then he pulls me to the spot next to him.

"Remember this slide?"

"How could I forget?" I blush, remembering our first "real" kiss here four years ago. Memories of that night begin to overwhelm me—too wonderful to ignore. So, I decide that perhaps sitting isn't the answer. Instead, I climb up the steps and slip down the tiny slide, feet first. When I reach the bottom, I slam into him and push off with my feet like I used to when we played slide bumper cars. He playfully falls off the slide and onto the wood chips below.

Then he sits up and stares at me. Really stares into my eyes. I look down at my bare legs.

"So what happened today?" Zachary asks, leaning back on his hands and tilting his head. "Why did you lose it at your locker?"

"I don't want to talk about it." I stare at the nearby swing set and take a deep breath. "Doesn't it seem like we were just here? Like the last few years just flew by?"

"Yeah . . . Remember when I dared you to jump off the swing set?"

"Yeah, and I stupidly listened to you. So I ended up having to get five stitches on my knee," I say, glancing at the puffy pink scar, a reminder of my recklessness.

"I didn't dare you to jump off when it was sky high! I meant, jump off when you were coming down. . . . Besides, you saw us all do it. You knew what I meant!"

"Well, you did come to the hospital with me . . ." I say, remembering how we waited in the emergency room together, playing Nintendo DS.

"Yeah, well, that was because . . ." Zachary stops himself.

"You can say it: because my mom wasn't there. Because she didn't show up at the hospital until we were already home."

Zachary diverts his eyes. "Yeah. But you know, I bet she wanted to check in on you. . . ."

"I wouldn't be too sure about that." I pause. The sense that I've been officially abandoned by my mother begins to overwhelm me. Suddenly, I look down at my feet and spot a penny on the ground. I can't resist. "Want a penny?" I pick it up and attempt to hand it to Zachary. He backs away.

"Oh no. I fell for that once already." He takes another step back.

"You mean when you were seven? It was your idea to throw it up and catch it in your mouth."

"You wish. It was on a dare from you!" Zachary grins, showing off his dimple.

"Oops . . ." I wince. "Sorry about that."

"You better be sorry—I had to have my stomach pumped." He rubs his hard abs like it still hurts, but it's clear that he's not mad. "The worst part was that my dad was having one of his 'episodes,' so your dad had to take me to the hospital."

"My mom was working and your dad was drunk—that's our normal world." I walk over toward the swing set and fall onto a black plastic swing. "What was with us and the dares anyway? You would think we would learn." I toss off my flip-flops and begin to pump my legs.

Zachary lights up. "I dare you to go to the prom with me."

"I dunno . . . our dares didn't always work out so well in the past."

Zachary shrugs. "I wouldn't say that. I guess we always

needed something to distract us from our messed-up families."

At that moment, I can't keep the truth a secret any longer. "My mom was supposed to take me dress shopping tonight. . . ."

"What happened?" Zachary asks, looking up.

I stop mid-swing. "Well, I'm here, aren't I? What do you think happened?"

He shakes his head, picks up another wood chip, and launches it across the playground. It pings off the fence.

"Yeah, but we always had sports," I say, pushing off again. "Except for me. I mean, what D-I program wants a high school benchwarmer?"

Zachary lets out a sigh. "All you have to do is claim that Amber's transfer was illegal. At least then you'll get some playing time."

I ignore him and swing higher and higher until I feel like I can touch the clouds.

"You know how the CHSAA goes bananas over illegal transfers. They would be all over this since Amber's such a stud. Seriously, Ky, she transferred on a whim her junior year. It breaks every rule out there. It's only fair that she should sit out the season." Zachary stands up, walks behind me, and begins pushing me even higher. "All you have to do is expose Amber for who she really is. Even if it's not true, Amber will be so tied up with investigations, she'll miss most of, if not the entire, rest of the season."

I nod ever so slightly, as if I might consider it, just to end the conversation. Even if accusing Amber would give me the opportunity to impress some D-I scouts, there's no way I'm going to the school board and being like, "Ummm . . . hello, I know you don't know me, but there's this girl—Amber McDonald—on my softball team, and I think her transfer here was illegal. So, yeah, you should investigate. It all sounds really shady to me." I might be mean, but I'm not *that* mean.

I change the subject. "Are you going to Vi's party tomorrow night?"

"Only if you are . . ." Zachary grabs the sides of my swing and pulls me to a stop. When my swing halts, he squats in front of me. Out of nowhere, he exclaims, "I'm so sorry."

"For what? Amber's transfer?" I ask, kicking some wood chips with my bare feet.

"No . . . Well, I am sorry to see how softball is turning out for you this year. But what I meant is I'm really sorry about those other girls last season."

I feel my shoulders stiffen. I kick one wood chip, then two, then three, then four.

"I miss this." He takes a step toward me, then closer and closer.

He's so close I can smell his mix of D&G and Tide.

"Talking to each other like we used to."

Me too, I think, but I don't dare say it.

"I've just been so happy that we're talking again. And that

we're on the prom court together. It's like everything is back to the way it should be. Everything is normal."

There's a silence between us. Zachary gently touches my heart charm. "I saw this a few weeks ago. I can't tell you what it meant to me when I saw you still wearing it." He grabs the clasp and slowly maneuvers it back behind my neck.

I touch the friendship bracelet I gave him on his wrist.

When I look up, he dives into my lips, tasting as always like peppermint gum. He kisses me hard and pulls me closer and closer. So close, I feel like we're one. Then he cups my cheeks. I love it when he, only he, touches my face. I move my hands to my favorite spot—his lower back. I pull him even closer.

The tingles turn to chills, shooting goose pimples down my legs. His hands move from my cheeks to the back of my head, then down my back. A cool ocean breeze runs through my loose hair.

When we finally break apart, Zachary and I are both breathless. "I need you, Kylie. I need you every day. You're the only one who makes my life right. And sometimes I wish I met you when I was older," he says, still staring into my eyes. "It just isn't fair to feel this way at seventeen."

I swallow a lump and stay silent. Nothing is fair anymore.

And I kiss him again.

thirty

"Party time!" Missy shouts, dragging a Fred Segal shopping bag out of her walk-in closet on Saturday night.

I fall on her thick white comforter and let out a deep breath. For a moment, I wish I could spend my night under the covers instead of at Violet's annual spring fling. Although it'll be fun to hang with my buds, I'm exhausted from all the stress from this past week. And frankly, after that kiss on the playground, there's someone else who I'd rather see . . .

I roll over and pick up a pale pink bottle of nail polish off the floor, sit up, and unscrew the cap.

"Word has it Violet's party is going to be ah-mazing. I cannot wait to take a dip in her hot tub. Just like last year. Me and Andrew . . . Ah . . ." Missy digs into her shopping bag and pulls out a periwinkle bikini. The suit matches her blue eyes.

I can't help it: I picture Zachary and me making out in the pool. Then, worried that Missy can see what I'm imagining, I stop myself and lazily drag the brush across my thumbnail.

"Why are you so beat anyway?" Missy asks, maniacally pulling assorted tops and shorts off hangers. She holds them up in front of her as she poses in front of the mirror. "Like?"

"I like that one. Good color." I point to a turquoise frilly tank that screams Anthropologie.

"Okay, so I have to ask . . ." Missy walks over and grabs the tank in question. "Did you finally find yourself a better catch?" She chuckles, shaking her head. "Actually, what am I saying? Anyone is a better beau than Zach."

I shrug, clutching my heart charm. "Nah, I think I'm off men. . . ."

Missy eyes me up and down. "Yeah, uh-huh," she says sarcastically. "I *really* believe you."

"Believe what you want." I shake out my polished fingernails.

"So, on that useless note, do you think I should switch to my white bikini?" Missy mischievously grins, holding up the string bikini she bought for Cabo last fall.

"If you're looking to be this year's prom princess. You'll definitely get votes with that see-through suit . . . Chloe." I giggle.

"Here. Try this on." Missy tosses a lavender sundress my way.

I keep my hands high to avoid ruining my nail polish as it lands on my lap.

Missy goes back to staring at herself in the mirror. "So, I'm sorry, Ky, I have to know. If you're off guys, where have you been the last two days? I texted you like a thousand times to hang out."

"Um . . ." I hold up the lavender dress by the hanger, careful not to smudge the polish.

"It *is* a new guy. Isn't it?" She sits down on the bed next to me, her eyes digging into my soul.

"Well, it's a guy. But he's not exactly new."

"Please don't tell me his initials start with a *Z* or an *M*."

I wince and look up at the oak-wood-trimmed navy ceiling.

"Oh my God! They do. You're seeing Zach again! Even after I told you again and again not to."

"Okay, so you're right. Congratulations. But I still don't think it's different from the whole you-and-Andrew thing."

Missy pulls off the cotton tee she was wearing over her bikini and violently tosses it on the floor with the rest of this week's wardrobe. She replaces it with the turquoise tank. Then she lets out a loud sigh. "I already told you—Andrew and I are different. He didn't win the challenge and it wasn't his idea. . . . And you know all of that. Plus, you have to give other guys a chance."

"Yeah. That's what you keep saying. Just like you thought Brett Davidson was into me."

"Wasn't he?"

"Uh, no. It seemed like he was going to ask me to prom, but I must have been imagining things because of your oh-so-helpful pep talks."

"What are you talking about?"

"You were there in class. You saw how our conversation ended. He's taking someone else."

"Zach probably threatened him."

I look out the row of windows that line the side of Missy's room. "Look. Zachary's been showing up when I need him. He gets me. We've been together since we were kids. I can't just walk away from him."

"Whatever, Ky." Missy rolls her eyes.

"And there's one more thing."

Missy freezes. "What is it?"

"I'm living in his guesthouse."

Her eyes widen to the size of softballs. "OMG! What?!? Does he come over at night? Are you guys—"

"No!" I squeak. "He's banned from coming anywhere near the guesthouse."

"So that's your dad's"—she mimes quotation marks—"*friend's* guesthouse?"

"My dad and Mr. Murphy have been friends for years," I say. "Technically I wasn't lying."

Missy flings a shoe across the room. It bangs against the wall. "Whatever, Ky. Just make the worst decision ever. No biggie."

"It wasn't my decision!"

"Yeah, living in his guesthouse wasn't—although, I mean, you could have lived here or something. But dating him again? That's definitely your decision."

"First of all, we're not really dating. . . ."

"You keep telling yourself that."

"We're not. We're taking things slow."

"Do you guys even know how to do that?"

"Miss, I just need you to trust me on this."

For a second, the room is silent. But then, Missy's answer shocks me. "Fine. Whatever makes you happy. Just don't get hurt again."

"Wait. What's with the sudden change of heart?"

Missy shrugs. "I just give up. I mean, I hate you guys together. But if being with him makes you happy, then who am I to stop you?"

At that moment, Missy gives me the second shock of the night. She comes over and gives me a hug. But then, not to be a total mush, she says something very much in character: "Okay Miss Zachaholic, let's get ready for Vi's spring fling!"

thirty-one

We pull up to the party in Missy's BMW and drive around the massive stone motor court, stopping at the line of uniformed valets. They take the keys from us, showering us with pleasantries, and we stroll up the winding walkway toward the Montgomerys' backyard.

Although I've been to Hannah and Vi's house before, I'm still shocked by the beauty of it. The yard is truly a spring fantasy. Two and a half acres of land are covered in tulips and daisies. A group of guys and girls are already playfully splashing around the pool. Another gang is enjoying a pickup game of volleyball in a sand pit, while a few freshmen, some of whom I recognize from softball tryouts, are involved in some serious badminton.

Behind the guests is a long granite walkway ending with a white picket fence and gate that opens up to a deserted section of beach. Tucked away from the house, in a parklike atmosphere, lies a beautiful patio area dotted with outdoor heaters and sheltered from the blowing sand by a transparent windscreen.

Lupe Fiasco's "Kick, Push" pumps from the booth behind

the pool. As expected, it's manned by Eva's boyfriend, Xavier (aka DJ Buzz Cut Cali).

My stomach swirls thinking about my own quasi-boyfriend, and how we agreed to meet by the pool.

As luck would have it, though, the first person who greets us *isn't* Zachary. "Hello, kitties," Hannah calls out. She's clad in a tight, neon-blue tank.

"Hey, girly," Missy says, hip-checking Hannah.

Hannah whispers something to Missy, and I can't be sure, but I think they're talking about the spaghetti strap lavender sundress that I ended up wearing with camel leather gladiator sandals.

I breathe out. I'm not going to let it bother me. "I'll see you guys soon," I announce. "I have to go find someone."

Missy glares at me, knowing who that someone is, and I can see she's trying to stop herself from screaming.

Surprisingly enough, she succeeds.

I wave goodbye and begin to make my way toward the pool. Along the way, I yell out, "Nice DJ!" to Eva, and am given warm hellos from Abby and Zoe.

Jessica stops me. "Love the sandals," she says.

"Uh, thanks," I say, looking over her shoulder in the direction of the pool. "I'll catch up with you later," I mouth. Then I continue walking.

"Looking good, Ky," a group of guys catcall.

I spin around and smile. Missy's oversized leather hobo grazes my back.

Being here in Vi's backyard, I feel totally in my element.

I pass through a group of B-Dubbers grinding to the beats. Dwight walks up to me and begins to move with me, dancing close. I can't help but join in for a few seconds. Then I twirl away and go to find Zachary.

When I finally make it to the pool, I hear Eminem's "Love the Way You Lie" start to blast from the speakers.

That's all right because I like the way it hurts.

I move to the wicked beat as I scan the area, my eyes finally landing on the adjacent hot tub. *There he is.*

There's no way I'm hitting the hot tub without first taking a dip in the pool. I toss my dress into my bag and step out of my sandals, adjusting my pale pink bikini top. Then I place my stuff on a nearby lounge chair and slink into the warm water.

A few guys turn around and whistle as I enter the pool. I wade through the water, inhaling the thick scent of chlorine as I pass a group of guys and girls chicken fighting.

I spot Zachary from across the pool, his back still toward me. *Perfect.* I can surprise him from behind.

I continue to push through the pool until I reach the edge of the hot tub. I stand behind Zachary, taking care that he can't see me. As I get closer, I realize he's leaning over chatting with someone.

Wait a second.

I take a closer look.

The pool is so crowded. Girls and guys hold red plastic

cups and dance and shout to the music. Everything is moving so fast that I'm dizzy. So dizzy I can't quite make out who he's talking to.

A girl?

No.

He leans closer to whomever he's chatting with. Then closer and closer . . . until . . .

He tries to kiss her.

What the hell?

My chest burns.

Just gonna stand there . . . Rihanna sings.

I thought he wanted to get back together. I thought he was sorry.

I love the way you lie. . . .

I grab Zachary by the arm and pull him toward me.

He stumbles a bit when he catches sight of me, his eyes as wide as saucers. "Kylie, uh . . . I thought you weren't coming for another hour."

Amber's eyes bulge behind him.

thirty-two

Without thinking, I turn around and snatch a red cup from Nick, who's standing stone-faced in the pool next to me. Then I launch the cup and everything in it at Zachary. The red punch drips down his face like lava.

"Kylie! What the . . . ?" he says wiping the red punch from his face.

"How could you do this?" I scream. Behind him, Amber slinks toward the side of the pool. Danielle hovers around me.

"I thought we were just keeping it casual," he shouts. At this point, he's shoveling pool water onto his face to attempt to wash out his eyes. Just like I thought: spiked. *Good. I hope it burns.*

I toss the empty plastic cup at him. He holds up his hands and blocks it so that it lands in the pool. "I love your spunk," he says, violently blinking his eyes.

"Shut up," I scream.

At the same time, DJ Buzz Cut Cali switches tracks.

"Hey, you said it yourself, we're just friends. That means we're not exclusive. And anyway you agreed with me. Remember? I said I wish I met you when we were older? I'm still young. You can't expect me to just be with one girl at seventeen."

"Not exclusive?! And too young?!" I scream back at him, feeling everyone's eyes on us. The pool is eerily silent and calm.

"Plus, I thought if I hooked up with Amy, I'd mess with her game." Zachary winks. "I was doing it for you."

"Her name is Amber, you moron!" I scream.

"It doesn't matter." Zachary sips from his red cup.

"You're no better than your dad!" I shout.

Zachary lowers the cup. "You're not seriously going to go there."

"Stay away from me. Don't call me. Don't come crying to me about your family. Don't even look at me. I hate you!" I scream. Then I turn around and push my way through the crowd, fighting to hold back the tears.

I wade as fast as I can to the side of the pool, use the concrete ledge to climb out, and stomp toward the chairs. I grab my bag, throw on my dress, and bend down to snatch up my sandals. I stomp across the concrete to the beat of Timbaland's "Morning After Dark," which is now pumping full blast from the speakers.

How could I be so stupid? Tears burn like fire in my eyes.

"Wait," someone yells from behind me.

I charge past my stunned friends, my vision so blurred with tears that I can barely make out their faces.

"Kylie, what happened?" Missy yells as I pass. "Where are you going?"

Phoenix cuts in front of me. "Is it true? Did you catch Amber with Zach?"

I push past her.

"Ky!" I hear Chloe from behind me.

I increase my speed.

Naturally, that's when I feel a tap on my arm. Amber stands drenched in front of me.

"Kylie, I'm so sorry," she shouts over the music, standing in a tie-dyed two-piece. Her red hair is piled high on top of her head.

I attempt to jockey past her, making sure I bump hard into her right shoulder.

"It wasn't anything, I swear," she continues, jogging next to me. "I swear I didn't do anything. We're teammates. The perfect pitching partners. I would never mess up our friendship."

I stop mid-stride. "Our friendship? Seriously? When have we ever been friends?"

"Kylie . . ." Amber begs, looking as if I just told her there's no such thing as Santa Claus.

"Just shut up, okay? And get the hell away from me!" I take off as fast as I can toward the beach, leaving Amber standing there, wet and shivering.

thirty-three

But strangely enough, telling Amber off isn't any kind of vindication. I fall onto the dry sand, the granules sticking to me. The tears I'd been trying to keep at bay stream down even more forcefully now. And with my clothes soaked—I didn't exactly have the opportunity to dry off—I'm freezing. I wrap my arms tight around my chest and use my bag as a blanket, laying it on top of me. My body shivers to the beats still pumping from Vi's party in the far-off distance.

I pull out my cell and scroll through my contacts. Finding the name of the one person whose voice I need to hear, I push "send."

Please answer. Please. Please. Just this one time.

One, two, three . . .

"You have reached the voice mailbox of Catherine Collins. Please leave your name and a detailed message and I will return your call as soon as possible. Thank you for calling and have a nice day."

Beep.

"Mom, I really need to talk to you. Please call me when

you get this. Things aren't working out for me in California anymore and my life is completely falling apart. Not that you would know. I really need you. And you *never* call me back. Plus, you blew me off for work. *Again.* Like you always do. Why do I even bother with you? Beats me. Call me. If you care."

I hang up and toss the phone into my borrowed bag. Then I stand up and take a step toward the ocean. Zachary and Amber's faces flash before me. I feel for my heart charm and pull, yanking it until the chain pops. Finally, I squeeze the charm in my palm and launch it into the crashing wave.

I'm done.

Okay, so maybe I picked the wrong time to declare my freedom. Or at least I didn't reason out all the details.

What was I thinking? Ditching the party, totally soaked? Running off without a ride?

I refuse to go back to find Missy. It doesn't matter that I'm chauffeur-dependent. There's no way I'm showing my face at that party again.

I resolve not to freak out. I throw Missy's bag over my shoulder and begin the trek toward my house. When I reach the sidewalk, an Audi slows down, pulling up beside me.

I don't let myself get nervous: I'm still in Vi's gated neighborhood. This person has to know me.

The passenger window rolls down and two hazel eyes peek out. I spot a pink-eraser topped pencil tucked above an ear. Not exactly a scary sight.

"Hey, look who it is. Kylie Collins, the ex-pitcher . . ." Rob Hamilton taunts. His squeaky voice is like nails on a chalkboard.

Then he reaches over and pulls out his silver voice recorder. "How does it feel to watch Amber steal your spot and your boyfriend?"

"Rob, I'm not in the mood."

"Come on, Collins, give the people what they want. A front-page story."

At that moment, I break.

"You want a story, Hamilton?" I pull on the door handle, taking a seat on the passenger side. "Tonight I'll give you a story that you'll never forget."

thirty-four

SOFTBALL SHAKE-UP AT BEACHWOOD ACADEMY

Junior Amber McDonald was poised to be the biggest star California high school softball has seen in recent years. But then, in a shocking move that rocked California softball, McDonald transferred midseason to Beachwood Academy from Southern California Upper Crest.

"During our first practice, she told me that she transferred because of a divorce," an unnamed teammate tells the *Sand Dollar*. "But I'm not buying it."

Last season, McDonald led the Upper Crest Cardinals to an impressive 18–2 record, shattering records by collecting six no-hitters, striking out two hundred, and walking only twelve.

"She's claiming the divorce was a hardship," the source adds. "And that it forced her to attend Beachwood. But don't you think it's a little convenient? There she was at Upper Crest, winning nearly every game. And suddenly, she decides to come to Beachwood, where we haven't won a championship in forever. She thinks we're pathetic. There must be something in it for her."

"Kylie, I'm home!" my dad calls out.

I jump out of my seat and slam my laptop closed, expecting to see a mob of B-Dub students holding torches and screaming, "Get Kylie!" It's been thirty-six hours since I gave Rob my so-called story, and I'm surprised that no one's barged through my door. (But just to be careful, I've closed all the blinds and turned off all modes of communication. I can't risk anyone sneaking a peek. Especially Zachary.)

Dad walks in through the kitchen door as I gather all of my belongings for school. He drops his blue yoga mat and squats to pet Kibbles, who greets him with licks. A woman, also in yoga attire, follows close behind. In one hand, she holds a black leather briefcase.

"Why is it so dark in here?" my dad asks, pulling up the blinds.

Clearly, he hasn't picked up on the fact that I've been hiding away since the night of the party. I ignore his question and offer up one of my own. "Who's that?" I point to the woman behind him. She smoothes out her chestnut ponytail.

My dad's shoulders relax. "Kylie, this is Bridget Fleishman from Calm Seas Realty. She also attends the yoga classes."

Yeah, I bet. If by classes, he means one-on-one sessions.

She holds out her thin hand. "Nice to meet you, Kylie." A whiff of perfume fills the kitchen air.

"What are you doing here?" I reply.

"Kylie, that's no way to treat a guest," my father answers.

Then he turns to little miss hot pants. "I apologize for my daughter's behavior."

"That's all right," Bridget replies. Her cloyingly sweet smile gets under my skin. She puts one hand on my dad's shoulder. "It must be hard for her, realizing that her house has been sold."

"Wait, what?! Our house has been sold?" I yell back. "What about Mom? Doesn't she get a say?"

"Your mother and I made this decision together," my dad answers, looking at me pityingly.

"Does that mean . . . ?"

"Yes, it does. We'll be moving again as soon as possible. Probably to a smaller, less expensive house farther inland."

Well, at least I don't have to live near Zachary anymore.

"How soon is soon?" I ask.

"Your father got an offer about two weeks ago and we just went into escrow."

"Huh?"

"Settlement. The period after which the house is officially sold," Bridget explains with a self-satisfied grin.

I glare at her. "So, wait. Let me get this straight. You two knew about this two weeks ago, and you're just telling me now?"

"It's complicated. We didn't want to tell you anything till we were sure," my dad replies.

"We?"

"Your father and I are together, Kylie," Twiggy says. As if it's the most natural thing in the world.

I turn to my dad. "So that's something *else* that you didn't tell me!"

My dad looks guilty. "It all happened so fast, and I didn't want to tell you until everything with the house was worked out."

"So you're saying that this random woman knows more about my life than I do!?"

"Kylie, you know that's not true. And besides, she's . . . uh . . ."

"I'm not a random woman," Bridget replies. This time her saccharine smile sends me over the edge.

"I can't take this anymore!" I scream. I grab my school stuff in a huff and stomp out of the house, slamming the door behind me. It's not until I step outside that I brace for the inevitable onslaught at school.

I stand at my locker before homeroom, scanning the hallways like a warrior scouting out his enemy. *What was I thinking the night of the party? Why would I spill to Rob Hamilton, of all people? Sure, Amber deserved it—she stole my spot and was about to suck face with my boyfriend. But . . .*

"Hey, Ky." Jessica meets me in front of my locker. "Are you okay? I saw you at the party with Zach. . . ."

"Oh. That. You know how Zachary and I are. It was nothing," I say, diverting my eyes from hers. "What's up with you? What are you reading?" I look at her books to see if a newspaper is peeking out among the notebooks.

"Huh?"

"You know, reading? I'm dying to read a good story. Maybe in the *Sand Dollar*?"

"Oh . . . Yeah, I heard there was supposed to be some big story this morning, but I haven't checked it out yet." She grabs my hand. "But forget about the *Sand Dollar*. Can you believe that our tournament is on Saturday? Followed by prom!"

"Yeah, it's pretty unbelievable. . . ."

"Hannah and Missy finished my dress last night. You should see it! It's amazing!"

I sigh as I shut my locker. "I can't wait to be totally and completely awed," I say. Jessica doesn't deserve any of the Kylie wrath.

"What does your dress look like?" she asks, walking beside me as I make my way to homeroom.

"I . . . uh . . . I . . . didn't get one yet," I say, still surveying the hallway. "Because I'm not—"

"What?! The prom is like less than a week away! What are you going to do?" Jessica screeches.

I shrug. As I'm about to tell Jessica that I've decided not to go to prom since I don't have a date, I hear deep heaving sobs.

"I can't believe someone would do this to me!" Amber shouts. Phoenix, Chloe, Nyla, Emily, and her buddy Danielle surround her.

Jessica takes off to join the sob fest.

"Did you see this?" Phoenix's eyes are the size of drink coasters. She holds up the latest copy of the *Sand Dollar.*

I shrug. "What?"

Nyla points to the front-page article. The headline "Softball Shake-up at Beachwood" stares back at me.

"It's horrible. Some unnamed teammate"—Sophia finger quotes—"said all these terrible things about Amber."

"Seriously?" I divert my eyes to the concrete floor.

"Seriously." Phoenix lowers the paper. Looking over her shoulder at Amber sobbing, she moves closer to me. "Did you do it?"

"What? That's a ridiculous thing to say. Of course I didn't do it!" I take off toward Amber and attempt to get involved with the group hug.

"Amber, I just heard. . . . I'm so sorry. . . ." I awkwardly tap her on the back of her long-sleeved ASA tournament tee.

Danielle steps in front of her before Amber can even move. She crosses her arms in front of her matching tee. "Do you honestly think anyone here doesn't know that you did this?"

"I don't know what you're talking about," I say, biting my bottom lip.

"Save it. Everyone knows you're pissed at Amber because she stole your spot and you caught her with Zach. And everyone knows that you're the most vindictive, horrible, ruthless girl when it comes to your boyfriend. Go away and spread your jealous rage somewhere else." She stands with her lips pursed.

Chloe steps in front of the group and stares at me. "Just go," she says.

Amber lets out another wail.

And, of course, that's when the loudspeaker announces, "Kylie Collins, please report to Coach Kate's office immediately."

thirty-five

Before I even make it to Coach Kate's office, she stops me dead in my tracks.

"What is this?" She holds out the *Sand Dollar*, pointing to the front-page headline. "Is this some sort of sick joke?"

I feel chills run up my back. "It's . . ."

Martie walks over and motions for us to take it inside to the offices.

Coach follows her, visibly annoyed. She signals me into the room, slams the door to her office shut, and throws the newspaper onto her desk. It lands next to her #1 COACH coffee mug. "No, 'It's not a joke'? Or no, 'This was the dumbest thing I've ever done, Coach'?"

Martie sits in a leather chair next to Coach's desk. She stares at me intently.

"I . . . I . . ."

"You what? Please, don't tell me that this was your way of getting back at Amber for taking your spot. In fact, Martie and I were just discussing what a long way your attitude has come since basketball season." Coach Kate lets out a deep breath. "But then today, I read the paper and see you're up to your old tricks." She twists her hair into a ponytail in a huff.

Martie adds, "This is completely inexcusable. I've already had to take a conference call this morning with the California High School Athletic Association."

"I didn't . . . ."

A line forms between Coach Kate's eyebrows. "I don't know what you could possibly say right now to make this right. This article is going to kill us. Our season. Our dreams. The future of the Beachwood Softball program. And I cannot believe that you took it upon yourself to humiliate Amber and this program by calling the school newspaper." Coach Kate snatches the mug from her desk and gulps her coffee.

"I never meant to. . . ."

"We know you sometimes react before you think. But Kylie, this time you went too far," Martie adds.

"But . . . I didn't. . . ."

Coach Kate looks at Martie.

"We figured you would deny your involvement," Martie says.

I look down and contemplate fessing up—anything to help erase the extreme guilt weighing on my chest.

"Although I really want to believe that you had nothing to do with this mess, it's hard for me to conceive that you wouldn't be out for blood when it comes to Amber." Coach rolls back in her chair.

"Coach, I swear I . . ." I meet Coach's eyes again.

"My first instinct is to expel you from the program immediately." Coach pauses. "Unfortunately, however, as the source is unnamed, I have no actual proof of your involvement. And, as much as it pains me to say this, I can't toss a player off the team based on suspicion."

I look up. *What? She can't?* My initial urge to fess up flies out of my mind like one of Nyla's home runs over the complex fence.

Martie holds up the newspaper. "Because of this, the CHSAA is asking us to hand in our books, Amber's tuition payment information, and even receipts from the bookstores, like we're criminals. They told me that as of today, Amber's hardship application has not been approved and that they're launching a full investigation into her transfer."

I gulp. *Thanks, Zachary, for the great idea.*

Coach Kate takes another long sip from her mug. "And now—I can't believe I'm going to say this—but since Sophia is absent and I have no one else who can pitch at the varsity level, I have to go against my better judgment and"—she glances at Martie—"let you start you on Thursday."

What?!?

Coach continues. "Because of this article, you got your way. Congratulations."

My stomach does somersaults. I should be happy, but it all feels horribly wrong.

"Remember, this is only until Amber's suspension is revoked. And if we find out you were somehow complicit in this, you'll be yanked off the team so fast you won't know what happened. Now, go." She points to the door.

I nod and slink out of Coach's office.

thirty-six

Things aren't much better by the time we take on Oceanview at our complex on Thursday. For the past two days, my teammates have been giving me the silent treatment during practice. And I was "asked" not to come to a meeting held to discuss the CHSAA's investigation into Amber's transfer. And to a dinner at Abby's house held to celebrate our participation in the Desert Invitational tournament. And even to our pre-game meeting.

I launch a warm-up pitch at Zoe before the top of the second inning.

Finally, Nyla breaks the deafening silence behind me. "Play's at first," she calls out.

I receive the ball from Zoe. She glares at me and I feel a pain in my chest. Even Zoe, who witnessed everything that happened between me and Zachary, isn't talking to me.

Coach Kate relays the sign.

Zoe holds down five fingers.

I shake off the rise ball.

I hate that pitch. If I only had Amber's natural talent with the rise ball—or better yet, if I only worked harder on it—I wouldn't be in this mess.

Zoe shows me an outside fastball. I wind up and snap my wrist, firing a fastball.

Smack.

"Strike," the umpire calls out.

A couple of fans clap. The rest sit on the bleachers with their arms tightly crossed. Even the crowd is pissed.

Zoe tosses me the ball and I walk back to the mound. The *K* signs in center field have disappeared since the day the article broke, along with the lacrosse team. Only one lonely sign, SAVE BEACHWOOD SOFTBALL—REINSTATE AMBER MCDONALD, remains.

"Play's at first," Nyla repeats.

Zoe gives me the sign for the drop ball.

I set up, push off the rubber, roll my hand over the ball, and short step toward Zoe's glove.

Dong.

The ball sails out toward center field. Chloe charges forward and catches the ball by the fence. She rolls it toward me as she jogs. I run out toward her with my glove hand up for a slap. She immediately runs the other way.

Just then, Phoenix runs past me.

"Hey, Phoenix!" I say, holding up my hand.

She ducks her head and continues in the opposite direction.

Clearly, no one's interested in reveling in how well

we're doing. *Or at least not with me.* I jog over to the dugout and find a bunch of my teammates consoling Amber. Their togetherness—which has been nothing short of unstoppable these past two days—stands in direct contrast to how alone I feel.

"Don't worry. You'll be back out there in no time," Chloe says, glaring at me from out of the corner of her eye.

"I heard that Coach might have this mess straightened out by Friday," Phoenix says, trying to calm Amber down.

"Yeah. Just in time for the Desert Invitational," Nyla adds.

"Hang in there. We're going to need you for the tournament," Danielle says, squeezing Amber's shoulder.

Once the team has gathered in front of the dugout, Nyla shouts, "Hits on three. One, two . . ."

I add my hand to the cheer.

Nyla stops counting. She looks at me, then my hand.

I pull it away.

A chorus of "Hits" breaks out, but I'm not among the screaming voices.

One thing's for sure: *I need to figure out how to make this right.*

thirty-seven

A few hours later, my mortification reaches an all-time high when the Beachwood school bus drops me off in front of Zachary's house. It's been years since I took the bus, and it's even more humiliating than I remembered.

I toss my Under Armour bag over my shoulder and drag myself across the aisle, down the three rubber steps, and out the door. Once I reach the street, I take a deep breath and wonder if this is how I'll spend the rest of high school—in total self-induced purgatory.

I trudge through the wrought-iron fence gate, keeping my back to Zachary's house. Then I shove my key into the lock and head directly to my room, passing Kibbles along the way. As I'm about to fall onto my duvet, I notice a huge box sitting there.

What the?

Kibbles, who followed me into my room, barks at me to open it.

I tear open the package and find myself face-to-face with a long, black Marc Jacobs garment bag. I quickly pull out the garment bag, accidentally sending a small white envelope fluttering to my bed. KYLIE is written on it in calligraphy. I rip it open. My mother's handwriting stares out at me.

Dear Kylie,

Every prom princess deserves a dress to match. And here's yours! Sorry we didn't get to shop together this year, but I know you'll wow the crowds in this gown. You're my daughter, after all! Just remember what you learned from the pageant circuit—keep those shoulders back and your chin high. Oh, and say hi to your friends for me!

Love, Mom

I toss the note on my dresser. *She didn't forget!*

Then I take a deep breath and unzip the bag. Inside I find a long ebony strapless gown. I pull it out and admire the open back. As I turn the dress this way and that, the silver shimmery accents glisten. *It's beautiful. . . .*

I strip off my softball uniform and step into the silk fabric. The dress is smooth against my skin. Looking up at myself in the mirror, I tug on my hair band. My hair falls across my shoulders in soft honey-blonde waves.

Kibbles sits at attention by the mirror, watching me.

I smile at her, thinking that if dogs could talk, she'd tell me how awesome I look.

And yet, despite how perfect it all is, something about this dress just seems wrong.

I pick up my mom's note and think about how prom was supposed to go—with my mom, with Zachary, with my friends. Naturally, that's when my dad peeks his head into my room.

"Hey, cupcake," he says. Then he takes a good look at me. "Sweetie, you look stunning. Where'd you get the gown?"

"Mom," I tersely reply.

"Oh. So that's what was in that box." He slowly walks around my room, glancing at my pictures. "Nice one of you and Missy," he says, pointing at a picture taken after we won the basketball championship.

"Yeah, it's okay." I place the torn box on the ground. Kibbles takes this opportunity to snatch it with her mouth, even though it's larger than she is, and run out of the room.

My dad and I stew in silence. But then, after a while, I have to say something. "So, uh, shouldn't you be getting back to Bridget?"

Dad removes the photo from the wall. "No, that's okay. She's not here." He pauses, staring intently at the photo. "I think I may have sprung her on you too quick . . . or maybe not quick enough. I don't know. I was never good with these things. Your mother . . ."

"Yes?" I take the photo from him and place it back where it belongs—on the collage I made in honor of our three-peat. I'm surprised that as I'm doing this, he doesn't say anything in response. It doesn't take long for me to realize that, once again, I'm going to have to be the one who breaks the silence. "Yes, Dad? What about Mom?"

"Oh, it's just that I know things haven't been easy for you since she left for New York." He pauses, taking a deep cleansing breath.

I stare at his yoga tee.

"And I know that I probably only added to the severity of the situation by moving out of the house, refusing to use most of the money from your mom, and setting up residence here." Again, he pauses. "Plus, there's the whole Bridget thing. . . ."

I move my gaze to my dad's tired eyes. "Honestly, Dad, the Bridget thing is really only the tip of the iceberg."

"Still, it must be hard for you." He puts his hand on my shoulder.

At that moment, I break.

I shake his hand off me. "Yeah, Dad, it is. But it's not nearly as hard as you pushing Mom away or you deciding to be all high and mighty about our finances or—"

Dad cuts me off. "Kylie, I'm sorry for all of that."

"Let me finish, Dad. Did you think that maybe moving into my ex-boyfriend's guesthouse might be the worst thing you could do for me?"

"Yeah, of course I figured it'd be challenging. But—"

"But you didn't think that was enough of a reason to stay in our house a bit longer?"

"I thought our not being there would make it easier to sell. Besides which, there were all those memories of your mother. . . ."

"See! That's exactly what I'm talking about! You thought it was hard to deal with *memories* of Mom. But I have to deal with living twenty feet from Zachary! Not to mention being ripped away from the house I grew up in!"

"I know I've made some mistakes in my life, Kylie. And I guess I figured that you and Zach have always been friends. . . ."

"But have you looked around? We're not exactly friends anymore." I take enough steps away so that my bed is between us.

"I knew you were going through a rough patch. . . ."

"It's more than a rough patch."

"I guess I didn't really understood that."

"Of course you didn't understand it! You weren't looking! Mom would have looked. . . ." My voice trails off. "At least, she would have before. And don't you dare go saying that—"

"You're right. She would have."

"What?" My mouth drops. *Did my dad actually say something good about my mom?*

"I said that you're absolutely right. Before she took this job, she would have noticed. And I was too caught up in my own stuff to really see what was happening with you."

I look up at my dad. His eyes are red.

"But I won't make that mistake again."

"Yeah? Really?" I ask. My voice is tinged with sarcasm. "How are you going to manage that?"

"Kylie, you're my only daughter. I want to know what's going on in your life."

"Let's just say: a lot."

"Cupcake, please. I want to help." He grabs my hand from across the bed.

I look down at his hand in mine and the words tumble out before I can stop them. "Well, for starters, Zachary and I are done for good."

"So that's why you've been so mopey lately. . . . I should have known."

"Dad, that's only the beginning. There's tons more where that came from."

"Okay, so tell me."

"I'm sure you don't really want to hear it."

"No, I do—"

"And besides, don't you have a yoga class to get to? Or some sun salutations to do with *Bridget*?" I infuse her name with every ounce of annoyance I possess.

"Sweetie, none of that matters. Bridget is great, sure. And I find yoga enormously relaxing. But at the end of the day, you're the one I care about. You're the one who I want to be there for. Who I should have always been there for. I . . ." He stops short when a tear escapes down his cheek.

Finally, I decide to confess. "I lost my starting spot on the softball team, Dad."

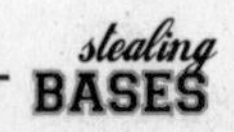

"What!? That's impossible. You're . . ."

"Save it. It happened. That's why I didn't want you coming to my games. And I made a complete mess of things afterward. With my teammates, with my friends, with my coaches . . ."

"Honey, I'm sure it can't be that bad. . . ."

"Dad. It's bad."

"Well, they'll have to forgive you eventually. You've known all of them for years."

"And what if they don't?"

"They will."

"Your saying that isn't exactly much comfort. How do you know?"

"I know because we're having this conversation." Another tear escapes. This time, it trails down his other cheek.

"What's that supposed to mean?" I ask, wiping away a tear of my own.

"Well, we're talking. For once. And we haven't talked like this in so, so long."

"Yeah, well, like I said, I've been busy."

"No, honey, don't go down that road. Don't pull away. What I'm saying is that you're opening up to me. And for you to do that, you must have forgiven me. At least at some level, deep down. And if you could forgive me for turning your life inside out . . . Well, there's no way that what you did to your friends was nearly as bad as what I did to you." He sits down on my bed, his head in his hands.

Still in my dress, I scooch next to him, placing one hand on his shoulder. "Dad, you didn't mean to do anything to me."

He looks up. "That doesn't matter. I'm your father, and I should start acting like one." He puts his arms around me, bringing me in for a warm embrace. And then he just holds me there, making all the pain wash away.

"I love you, Kylie," he says, squeezing me tighter.

My reply escapes before I can even stop to think. "I love you too, Dad."

And in that moment, I realize: I do love him, yoga shorts and all.

I always have.

thirty-eight

My dad stands in my doorway, about to leave my room, when he stops and says, "I got so caught up with our talk that I almost forgot to tell you: Missy's outside waiting for you."

What? Missy? I thought she dropped me like last fall's blazer trend. *Just like everyone else.*

"Do you want me to send her in?"

"Sure," I say. My stomach drops as my dad walks out of the room. *What if she's only here to reprimand me?* After the chat with my dad, I'm finally feeling a little bit better. I don't think I can take any more criticism.

As I'm thinking this, I realize that I'm still in the gown my mom sent over. Quickly, I slink out of it, shove it back into the garment bag it came in, and throw on a pair of B-Dub sweats and an ASA tee.

A moment later, Missy walks in. The first thing she does is look around the room. I can see that she's thinking about how tiny it is.

She doesn't say anything.

"So . . ." I begin. "You're here."

"Of course I'm here," she says, running her hand along my dresser. "I couldn't not come to talk to you, could I?" She stops when she notices the same photo my dad pointed to earlier. "We've been best friends for years, haven't we?"

"Yeah, but that was before you got yourself a new best friend." I look over at the Marc Jacobs garment bag, now hanging awkwardly in my closet, and think about what should have been.

"First off, you know Hannah is *not* my new BFF. Secondly, I figured, Kylie's one pissed off girly tonight. Understandable after everything you've been through."

"I'm surprised you're not taking Amber's side. Isn't that what the whole school is doing?"

"Ky, I don't know if you spilled to the *Sand Dollar* or not. But God knows, I'm no saint. So who am I to judge?" She sits on the edge of my bed.

I turn to face her. "You mean that?"

"Do you even have to ask?" She smiles mischievously. "But if you wanna tell me what *really* happened . . ."

"Nah, I'll let the mysterious source remain anonymous."

"Suit yourself." Missy sighs. "But you know, I've been thinking. I've been working with Hannah for like two months and I know more about her than I've ever known about you." Missy lies on her stomach, resting her chin against the back of her hands. "And we've been best friends since birth."

I roll my eyes. "If you think telling me about your new BFF is really helping me, you might want to consider another strategy."

"Ky, how many times do I have to tell you? Yeah, there's a lot more to Hannah than I thought. But she's not my best friend. You are."

"So then why have you been spending *all* of your time with her lately? And why is she the only one you ever talk about?"

"Because I *need* her."

"No one needs Hannah."

"I hate to admit it, but *I* do. She's more talented than me, and if I want to stand out when I apply to college, she's really my only hope."

"Fine, whatever. But it doesn't seem like you're just using her anymore. It seems like you two are actually friends."

"I never thought I'd say this a few months ago, but yeah, we are."

"So then I'm right." I cross my arms.

"Ky, she's a friend, yeah. But . . ." Missy pauses. "She's not you."

"You mean that?"

"Duh. Of course I do!" She bolts upright and throws her hands up in the air. "But seriously, Kylie, *you're* the one who usually shuts *me* out. I didn't even know about your parents' divorce until my mom told me. And then I didn't find out about your moving to Zachary's guesthouse until the night of the party. Who doesn't tell their best friend that kind of stuff?" She takes a deep breath. "So are you going to tell me what else is going on?"

"I wouldn't even know where to begin."

"How about we start with your favorite topic: your mom. Is she permanently in New York now?"

"I don't even know. She said it was only temporary, but I haven't seen her since Christmas. And apparently she didn't even care that my dad just sold our old house."

"He did?"

"Yeah. Just—"

Missy interjects. "So does that mean you'll be leaving *casa de Murph*?"

"Yup. My dad hopes to move somewhere further inland where there will probably be solar panels and a giant compost pile in the backyard."

"Crazy."

"I know. But what's even crazier is that my mom never calls me back, so I haven't even gotten to talk to her about it."

"When was the last time you guys spoke?"

"Let's see . . . There was the time she canceled our shopping trip via text. And then today I got a prom dress from her in the mail."

"Hold on a sec. That's good, isn't it? I thought that's what you wanted."

"Sort of. But it was more about something for us to do together, you know?" I walk over to my dresser and pick up the discarded card. I quickly glance at it one more time and then hand it over to Missy. "And the way she worded this card—it's like the only thing she cares about besides work is my being named prom princess."

Missy scans the card. "Well, she definitely still loves you."

"Maybe." I walk over toward my window and peek out the blinds. Zoe and Zachary are playing a pickup game of basketball in their backyard court.

A bolt of lightning rips through my stomach.

Missy stands next to me. "You really can't escape Murph, can you? No wonder you've been freaking out."

I shut the blinds. "I've been freaking out about Zachary because I didn't want to believe that he changed."

Missy turns toward me. "I'm sorry—you really have been dealing with a lot of that lately." She pauses. "Change, I mean."

"No kidding."

Missy pushes out her lip-glossed bottom lip. "Aww . . . but that's exactly why you should've told me about everything! I could've helped."

"Miss, it's humiliating enough to be in my situation without all of Beachwood knowing."

"I would never tell anyone, Ky." Missy places her hand on my shoulder. "I can't believe you don't trust me."

"I don't trust anyone right now."

"You trust Zach. . . ."

"I *did* trust him. But that's different. He wouldn't talk

about me. Or at least there was a time when he wouldn't have . . ."

"Yeah, he might not talk about you, but he'll rip your heart out and stomp on it," she says, pulling me down to the hardwood floor. We both sit cross-legged, our knees touching. "You know sometimes when you think people are talking about you to be mean, they're really just worried about you."

"Easy for you to say. Your life isn't falling apart." I stare at my painted toenails.

"Yeah, I'm really lucky that things in my life are pretty good right now, but—"

I cut her off. "Which is exactly why—"

She does the same to me. "Ky, let me finish." She takes a deep breath. "I meant what I said—there are people out there who want to help you, but you just turn away."

"Even if you're right, and I'm not saying that you are, all of that was before the article hit."

"Come on, Ky. Everyone is pretty used to your Murph madness. I'm sure they'll find a way to get over it."

"I doubt it. Everyone hates me. Especially my teammates."

"They won't forever."

I roll my eyes. "Have you been hanging out with my dad?"

"Nah, I'm not *that* good of a friend." Missy giggles. "But seriously, even if you were the source—and like I said, I don't care if you are—you just have to find a way to make it up to people."

I push myself off the ground and walk over to my closet, grabbing hold of the Marc Jacobs garment bag. "Sometimes that doesn't work."

Missy stands up and maneuvers her way around my bed to stand next to me. "Yeah, sometimes it doesn't. But you're Kylie Collins. You have to try."

Missy pulls the garment bag from my grasp and lays it out on my bed. "So this is the dress your mom sent you, huh?" She unzips the bag and brushes her fingers against the soft material. Then she picks it up by the hanger and gently twists the dress to admire the detailed back.

Satisfied, Missy places the dress back inside the garment bag. "So your mom mailed you the dress you were supposed to pick out with her. . . ."

"Yeah, that's pretty much what happened. But it doesn't matter. I'm not even going to prom now anyway."

"Uh, hello? Yes you are. You can't bail on me now."

"It's not you that I'm bailing on. It's my life."

"How about instead of doing that, you try an easy fix." She walks over to my bag and pulls out my cell phone. Then she wraps her arms around me in a big hug. When she pulls away, she places the phone into my hand and says, "You know what to do to make this right." Then she leaves.

For a split second, I stare at the phone in my hand. Then I make my decision.

thirty-nine

After pre-calc the next day, the hallway is abuzz with prom chatter as I walk toward the locker room to dress for our final game before the big Desert Invitational tournament. I adjust the strap of my softball bag and spot Jessica and Abby staring at a copy of the *Sand Dollar*.

Here it goes.

"Hey." Taylor steps in front of me, holding a copy of the newspaper. She hands it to me. "Good stuff," she says, beaming at me.

I look down. The headline, COLLINS COMES FORWARD, stares back at me.

Taylor continues. "At first, I thought you were blowing your cover just to trash Amber some more. But then when I read the article, I was shocked."

"You were?"

"Yeah! But then again, I remembered our talk in the locker room last season. I always knew you had it in you."

I hand the newspaper back to Taylor and the edges of my mouth break into a smile.

"No, you keep it," she says, holding up her hand.

My smile grows wider as Taylor rejoins Abby and Jessica. Abby gives me the thumbs-up.

I wave to her and walk into an unused classroom. Then I spread the newspaper out on a desk and read the article.

COLLINS COMES FORWARD

In a shocking move, junior Kylie Collins has decided to publicly identify herself as the unnamed source behind the recent *Sand Dollar* article "Softball Shake-up at Beachwood Academy." She has asked that her earlier statement, in which she accused fellow junior star pitcher, Amber McDonald, of an illegal transfer, be retracted and reports that, to her knowledge, McDonald's transfer did in fact meet California High School Athletic Association (CHSAA) requirements.

"I guess I was just jealous," Collins said from her home last night. "I was looking for a way to win my spot back."

Collins, also a nominee for prom princess, was Beachwood Academy Softball's starting pitcher for the last two consecutive years. Amber McDonald, an all-state selection last year, earned the starting spot for the Wildcats this year, following her transfer from Upper Crest Academy.

"Amber would never do anything illegal," Collins stated. "She's one of the nicest and most talented players I've ever known."

McDonald has no prior record of any previous infractions.

"It was wrong of me to accuse Amber," Collins continued. "I really hope she can forgive me for attacking her during a very sensitive time."

At press time, McDonald is suspended from play and scheduled to meet with the CHSAA on Friday to decide her fate. This suspension comes at a particularly trying time for the Wildcats—one day before the prestigious Desert Invitational tournament.

Okay, not so bad . . . It could have been worse.

I crumple the paper and am about to throw it—and hopefully this entire mess—into the garbage can when I see a note in the bottom right-hand column.

TO ALL STUDENTS:

Please note: publication of the *Sand Dollar* will temporarily be suspended as the Beachwood Academy administration looks into possible ethical violations on the part of its reporting staff.

So Rob Hamilton is in as much trouble as me. . . . There is some justice in the universe.

Convinced that I've read enough, I drop the newspaper into the trash and pick up my softball bag. I walk back into the hallway, about to resume my trek to the locker room, when Coach Kate pokes out her head from her office. "Kylie, we need to see you for a second."

Great. Here we go again.

I let out a deep breath and step in Coach Kate's office, ready to receive my punishment.

forty

Although Coach Kate and Martie were a little more understanding about my behavior after I spilled my guts, I've officially been benched now that Sophia is back at school. Can't say that I disagree with their verdict.

"Abby's hurt, Coach!" Phoenix yells, just before the third inning of our away game against Curtis High.

I watch in horror as the team surrounds Abby at second. Immediately, the trainers sprint to the outfield, their first aid bags in hand.

In that moment, I cease to care whether anyone's still angry at me. It doesn't even matter that tomorrow is the Desert Invitational. Abby—Zoe's best friend—is hurt. I jump off the bench and dash toward second base.

"What happened?" I ask. I spot Abby laid out on the orange dirt, grabbing her knee. Zoe bends over her, holding her hand.

"Abs was moving hard to cover second, but her foot got caught and she fell," Nyla recounts.

"Hope it's not her ACL," Phoenix says.

"That's horrible," Amber adds, peering over the group.

Abby scrunches her face as the trainers begin to work on her knee.

"Ohmigod, I hope she's okay," Emily says.

I call out to Abby, "We're here for you, Abs!"

She grimaces.

One trainer gently presses against the injury, and Abby cries out.

"Give her air!" the trainer shouts.

About three minutes later, an ambulance pulls into the complex, swings around, and backs up onto the side of the field. Two medics pile out and rush a gurney onto the field. They hoist Abby up and wheel her into the ambulance. She holds out her hand, clinging to Zoe.

Zoe looks at Abby and then back at the team. And then, all of a sudden, it's like she has an epiphany. "She's not going to the hospital without me!" she announces.

Coach Kate turns to Emily. "Be honest with me. Has your wrist healed enough for you to play?"

Emily nods her head yes.

"Okay, then, I'll reinstate you as catcher," Coach replies. Coach motions for one of the trainers to quickly examine her.

"So that means I'm free to go?" Zoe asks.

Coach Kate shrugs. Clearly, she's had enough.

Chloe rushes forward to Coach Kate. "Forget about catcher. Who's going to play second?" she asks, scanning our remaining teammates.

"Danielle, you're in." Coach motions to second base. Instantly, Danielle's usual swagger is replaced by a look of panic. She's barely seen a second of playing time all season.

I hang my head and drift back toward my spot on the bench.

After today's meeting, Kibbles is more likely to play second than me.

"Poor Abby," a voice says. I turn to my left and see that Amber is sitting next to me on the bench. (Coach can't reinstate her until after tonight's official CHSAA hearing. So, *Sophia* of all people is pitching.)

"Yeah, I know, it's terrible," I reply, shocked that Amber is talking to me. "I can't get over all the injuries we've had this season."

"I know! First Emily and now Abby," Amber says.

"At least Emily is feeling better." I nod to Emily at home plate.

"Yeah, but Abby's never gonna get to play at tomorrow's games." Amber shakes her head.

"Well, hopefully you will." I attempt to be cheerful.

"Yeah, I think it'll be okay. . . ." Amber trails off. "The CHSAA really doesn't have anything to hold against me." She pauses.

"Listen, Amber. I'm so sorry that I said those things about you."

"Why did you?" Amber asks, confusion written on her face. "I thought we were friends."

"I shouldn't have. But I was just so envious."

"You were envious . . . of me?" Amber's expression looks dubious.

"Yeah, of course." I shrug.

"But you're Kylie Collins, Beachwood Academy superstar."

"I was 'Kylie Collins.' And you're the starting pitcher."

"I thought that stuff didn't bother you. We've talked since the roster was announced and everything seemed okay."

"It wasn't."

"Why didn't you say anything?"

"What was I gonna say? That I'm desperate to go to UCLA? That I wanted my spot back?"

Amber doesn't say anything in response.

"It's not like you would have given it to me."

Amber cocks her head to the side, looking more thoughtful than I've ever seen her. "No. But it would've been good to know."

I pause. "I've been hearing a lot of that lately."

"What?"

"That I should be honest with people about what I'm feeling. That I shouldn't keep everything inside." Fire burns in my stomach. "That's why I went to the paper with the retraction. I couldn't let the lie go on."

"Thanks for that," Amber says.

"You don't have to thank me," I say. "I was wrong to

embarrass you in the first place. And I should never have tried to manipulate the situation. It was the least I could do."

"But I know what it must have looked like—with Zach at the party. Not that anything happened . . ."

"I know that now. And honestly, I should have realized it then. You're not that type of person."

"No, I'm not."

We both stop talking as the opposing team scores another run. A collective sigh streams forth from the Beachwood fans.

I break the silence. "Amber, I never would have said this before all this crazy stuff happened, but can we be friends?"

Amber gives me a squeeze. "Of course! That's all I ever wanted for us."

I nod in Danielle's direction. "Do you think she'll allow it?"

"Uh . . . she'll get over it eventually." Amber giggles.

"Okay, so now that we know I'm safe from Danielle, I have to tell you something."

"Umm . . . okay."

"My mom lives in New York," I spill.

"What?" Amber obviously has no idea what I'm talking about.

"My mom left us. Me and my dad." I let out a deep breath after hearing the truth.

No more saying she works in New York. She left us. Plain and simple.

"Oh my God." Amber's eyes fill with concern. "I'm so sorry."

Feeling a lump in my throat, I turn my attention toward the field. "I'm okay. I just wanted you to know. That's all."

I feel Amber's hand pat my back. Although my first reaction is to move away, I stay put.

"So that's why you clammed up when I told you about my parents' divorce?" she asks, her hand still on my back.

I nod.

Another opposing player crosses the plate.

"Come on, girls. Smart choices!" Coach Kate yells.

"I told Coach Kate and Martie about that at our meeting today. After they saw my retraction, they could've suspended me from the team. But I think they appreciated hearing about why I've been so . . . off."

"That totally makes sense!" Amber replies.

"Honestly, I'm lucky I'm even on the bench today. Coach Kate had fair grounds for throwing me off the team."

Amber's mouth opens like a nutcracker. "But they never would have done that! You made a mistake."

"Yeah, and it's one I'll always regret."

"Cheer up! You're on prom court, remember?"

"No, actually, I'm not. I had to step away."

Amber gasps. "The prom court and softball? That's horrible. You poor thing."

"There are worse things . . ." I say, gazing out toward home plate as the opposing team scores another run.

Amber's bottom lip juts out. "Please tell me you're still going to the prom."

"No, not this year," I say, blinking as tears form in my eyes. "But it's not just because of prom court. With the whole Zachary thing, I'd already decided that I didn't want to go."

Crack. An opposing player sends the ball sailing over the left field.

Coach Kate throws her clipboard on the grass in frustration.

Amber moves her hand from my back to my arm. "But at least you still came close. You know, with the court and everything. No one can take that away from you." She beams. "I've always wanted to be prom princess. And you almost did it."

I look at Amber. "Well, if anyone deserves to be prom princess, it's you."

Her face lights up. "Aww, Ky. You're the best."

I wouldn't go that far.

forty-one

The next morning, the Beachwood Academy bus pulls up at the Desert Invitational tournament parking lot in San Bernardino. We unload the bus one by one. I take a step onto the lush grass and breathe in the hot, dry air. The grounds crew is still raking the fresh orange dirt, and another man is putting the finishing touches on the chalk lines in the batter's box.

I throw my softball bag over my shoulder and am about to head over to the team room with the other girls (many of whom are chatting about tonight's prom as much as they are about the Invitational) when I hear Coach Kate call out to me. "Kylie, can I talk to you for a sec?"

"Sure, Coach." *It's not like I'm actually going to be part of today's game anyway.*

"So, Kylie, I can't believe I'm going to say this, but I was talking to Martie and we would like to reinstate you."

"You'd . . . *what*?" I check my ears to make sure I'm hearing her properly.

"You showed tremendous courage issuing that retraction.

And we think that given that, and your recent honesty about your home life, you deserve another shot."

"You do?" My mouth drops.

"Yes, we do. But please know that we will not be so forgiving the next time you pull a stunt like that."

"I totally understand. Won't happen again," I say in a rush.

"As I said, it better not."

"Coach, may I ask: What changed your mind?"

"Actually, it was a who. Martie and I met with Amber at the CHSAA hearing last night. After the committee dropped the charges against her, she made a convincing argument in support of your reinstatement."

"She did?"

"Yes, you're very lucky to have a friend like her."

"I know," I reply. And it's true: *I am*. But then it hits me. "Coach, if Amber will be taking the mound, what position will I be playing?"

"Oh, right. About that. Martie and I discussed it, and we think that with Abby's injury, it would be best for the team if you play second base."

"Oh."

"Is that a problem, Kylie?"

"No, I'm just surprised. That's all."

"You shouldn't be. Martie tells me that you're quite the second baseman for your ASA team."

"Yeah, I guess. . . ."

"So, does that mean you're not interested in playing second?"

"No. No. I am! I'm thrilled!"

"Good. Go suit up with your teammates."

The words tumble out in a rush. "Will do! Thank you so much for this opportunity. I won't let you down."

I take two steps in the direction of my teammates when I hear Coach Kate pipe up again. "And Kylie . . ."

I turn around. "Yes, Coach?"

"Please know that this does not mean you've been reinstated to prom court. There has to be some punishment for your behavior."

The air sucks out of me like a balloon. But then reality strikes. "You know what, Coach? Just two minutes ago I thought I'd be watching three games go by without seeing any playing time." I pause, mustering more maturity than I thought I was capable of. "I'll take what I can get."

Hours later, the Desert Invitational tournament is in full swing and Beachwood is that much closer to saving the softball program. We won the first two games by five and are now squaring off against the reigning champions, Santo Bay, in the tournament final.

"Going to first. One out," Nyla shouts from shortstop during the top of the seventh inning. Since we won the pregame coin toss, we're the home team.

I've been on fire all day—going five for eight at the plate and sucking up everything at second. But right now, my skills hardly matter. The game is tied, zip-zip. It's truly a pitcher's dual.

Santo Bay's stud pitcher, Steffi Norcross, digs into the batter's box from the left side. I take a step backward and set up to cover first base in case Jessica is pulled off the bag.

"Winning run at the plate," Santo Bay's side shouts. "You got it, Steffi!"

Amber takes her time filling in the mound.

I breathe in the scent of my leather glove. Then I rise onto the balls of my feet and squat into position, placing my glove out in front of me.

Amber sets up, winds, and fires a fastball.

"Strike," the umpire yells. (For the nine-hundredth time.) The scouts in the stands salivate.

Emily fires the ball back to Amber. Then she turns around and waves at Zoe and Abby, who sit in the dugout, Abby's leg in a soft cast.

"Hit the ball down the middle, make the pitcher bend a little. Make her"—the Santo Bay dugout claps twice—"eat some dirt!"

Amber sets up again and fires.

Steffi leans into the inside pitch, allowing it to graze her right hip.

"Dead ball," the umpire shouts, taking off his mask. He points to first.

Steffi smirks, tosses her bat toward her dugout, and jogs to first.

"Way to take one for the team!" the dugout shouts.

"Time." Coach Kate jogs toward the umpire.

"She leaned into it!" I shout to the field umpire as he jogs by.

"She hit me!" Steffi yells from first. "On purpose."

"If Amber wanted to hit you with a pitch, she would have hit you in the face," I shout at Steffi.

"Kylie, bring it in," Nyla yells from shortstop.

The infield gathers at the pitcher's mound.

"Hey, pitcher, what's the matter? Can't you stand a little chatter?" the Santo Bay dugout sings.

"Shut up," I say to Santo Bay. "This is BS!" I shout to my teammates. Then I stare at Steffi, who's rubbing out her hip.

"Remember what Coach Kate said. We have to keep our emotions in check in situations like this. Santo Bay is trying to rattle us. Let's just get the next two outs and get our turn at the plate," Nyla says. "Let's play our game."

We watch as Coach Kate gestures wildly at the umpire. Then she hangs her head and jogs back to the dugout.

"On three, team," Nyla says, bringing us together on the mound.

We shout "team" and jog back to our positions.

The next girl, number eleven, also digs in on the left side.

"Watch another drag or chance for a free ride," I shout, glancing at Steffi.

Nyla looks over at me and smirks. "Nice to have you back, Collins."

Then she shouts, "Hit and run," while watching the third base coach give the signs to Steffi and the girl at second.

Amber sets up and fires.

Out of the corner of my eye, I watch Steffi take off toward second. At the same time, the batter shortens up her swing and drags the ball to Phoenix at third.

I sprint toward second. At third, Phoenix bobbles the ball, finally picks it up, and launches it to me. I catch it at second, attempt to step off the bag, and twist to fire the ball at first. Before I can throw it, Steffi takes me out with her slide. I tumble to the ground, catching myself with my hands. The ball rolls out of my glove.

"Safe," the field umpire shouts behind me.

Nyla grabs me as I'm about to land one on Steffi's face. "Come on, Kylie. She's not worth it."

Then I remember—let it go.

Even though I'd rather let it go all over Steffi Norcross, this game is too important. I take a deep cleansing yoga breath and return to my spot at second. Steffi stands up and wipes the dirt off her uniform.

But not before I yell something that goes against my attitude re-do in Steffi's direction.

"One out," Nyla screams.

Amber sets up, nods, and fires from the mound.

The Santo Bay batter doesn't move as the ball whizzes past her.

"Strike!" the umpire yells.

The batter steps out. At the same time, Amber receives the ball and digs out her mound.

I watch as three recruiters in the stands drop their radar guns and furiously write on yellow notepads.

Although I don't want to, I can't help but feel a tad green. I mean, I'm still Kylie. Quickly, though, I shake it off.

I squat into position as Amber explodes off the mound. The ball spins and hits Emily's glove on the outside corner. The batter swings and misses.

"Strike two!" the umpire shouts.

Amber receives the ball once more and walks back to the mound.

"No balls, two strikes," the umpire says.

Just as Amber is about to take the mound again, I spot my dad in the stands. I still can't believe he came all this way. He's been watching me all day long. He gives me a thumbs-up.

I'm about to give him a little wave when I see Amber burst off the mound.

Smack.

A perfect rise ball lands in the center of Emily's glove. The umpire punches the air.

Our side goes wild. Another *K* sign is added to the left field fence behind me.

"Two outs, any bag!" Nyla shouts.

"See what happens when you cheat?" I say to Steffi at second.

"Whatever." She rolls her eyes. "I'll be crossing the plate in a few. Our best batter is up." Steffi sets up on the bag, ready to take off.

Zoe tosses the ball back to Amber.

Santo Bay's number four digs into the batter's box. She takes a deep breath and stares out toward center field. During her last two bats, she launched two balls to the fence. Luckily, we were ready for her.

I turn around and shout to the outfield, "Big bat."

"Give her room!" Coach Kate shouts. "Your way twice, Chloe!" Like me, Chloe somehow ended up starting after a season of benchwarming.

Amber sets up on the mound. She winds up and throws another rise ball.

Number four's eyes widen. She loads up and swings hard.

Smack.

The ball sails in between center and left field. It soars higher and higher.

Clang.

The ball smacks the fence. Steffi takes off. She's around third before Chloe can field the ball. Eventually, Chloe grabs it and launches it to Nyla. Nyla successfully catches the ball. But it's too late. Steffi crosses home plate.

Quick on her feet, Nyla fires the ball to Phoenix to keep the run at third. Phoenix runs the ball in to a stunned Amber.

This is not good.

"First or second," Nyla shouts. "Two outs."

"Batter up," the umpire shouts at the bottom of the seventh inning. At this point, Santo Bay leads by one.

Before I step into the box, I glance at the stands.

"Yay, Kylie! Woot woot!" I spot Missy, Tamika, Taylor, Eva, and Hannah on the bleachers. Each of them shakes a white and blue pompom.

I grin at my buds.

They came all the way to the tournament hours before our junior prom. Wow.

I force myself to concentrate. There'll be time to thank them later. I stare at Coach Kate. She gives me the drag sign. I'm not surprised. With Nyla up behind me, Coach is thinking, get me on base and hope Nyla hits a bomb.

I do my best to ignore the butterflies in my stomach. I step to the left side of the plate and dig into the batter's box. Then I hold my hand in a stop position to the umpire as I dig out the dirt.

"Watch slap," the catcher yells as I load my hands on the bat and set up in the batter's box.

Steffi winds up. Once her arm rotates toward her hip, I make my move, crossing my feet and stepping toward the pitcher. *Smack.* I make immediate contact. The ball skims over the first baseman's head. I take off toward first. Fortunately for me, the right fielder and the second baseman reach the ball at the same time. Confusion erupts and they lose precious seconds before the right fielder finally snatches the ball and fires it to first. Chalk puffs in the air as I step on the bag.

"Safe," the infield umpire shouts.

"Yes!" I pump my fist.

Our first base coach, Coach Jackie, slaps my hands. We both look at Coach Kate, who's in the process of touching her nose, forehead, and ear. Her movements are so quick, it's a good thing I've been studying the signs all season from my spot on the bench.

I adjust my helmet and prepare to sprint.

Nyla steps into the batter's box.

Santo Bay's coach shouts, "Big bat!" And his players arrange themselves accordingly.

Nyla stares at the pitcher.

She winds up.

I take my lead.

She launches a hard pitch.

Nyla watches the ball sail into the catcher's mitt.

"Strike," the umpire yells.

Nyla steps out and looks over at Coach. Coach Kate taps her nose, her ear, and then she drags her hand down the front of her thigh.

I nod. *Here we go. Hit and run.*

I straddle the bag and move my arms into position to run.

Nyla steps into the batter's box again and digs in. The pitcher begins her motion and whips her arm. At the same time, I take off for second.

Smack.

As I sprint, I look up and see the ball sailing toward the outfield. Santo Bay's left fielder turns around and takes off after it, but the ball is years behind her. I turn it on. Everything I've got. Every ounce of anger. Every tear. Everything.

Coach Kate is waving me home. As soon as I round third, I spot my friends on their feet up in the dugout. Their cheers echo throughout the stadium.

"Run home!" Coach yells.

I don't miss a beat. But when I reach home, Santo Bay's catcher stands there, blocking the plate like a soldier.

"Down!" my teammates scream.

My helmet bobs on my head with each step. I keep my eyes down and slide into home. I lie back, attempting to slip underneath the tag. The yellow ball lands in the catcher's glove. Dry dirt puffs like a cloud, gritty in my mouth. The catcher lays down the tag hard on my stomach.

But the ball isn't there.

"Safe," the umpire yells.

I stand up and pump my arms. Then I turn around to spot Nyla. Santo Bay's catcher retrieves the ball. She fires it hard to third. Nyla slides into third base. But the catcher misfires and the ball sails into left field.

Coach Kate jumps up and down, waving her arms for Nyla to sprint home. I stand behind home plate. *Will she make it?*

Nyla charges hard and slides headfirst into home. A huge dirt puff clouds my vision.

"Safe!" the umpire shouts.

The dust cloud clears and my teammates surround us in a mob of excitement. We fall into a human pile.

And just like that, it's like nothing bad ever happened.

forty-two

And from there, things only get better.

"Did I just hear that you're back on the prom court?" Missy asks, once I'm settled into the front seat of her car after our post-tournament celebration.

I gingerly place my MVP trophy on the floor in front of me. (It should really say "co-MVP." Amber also got one.) I choose my words carefully. "Guys, that doesn't matter. What matters is that you all were there for me today and that we saved Beachwood Softball."

Not surprisingly, they ignore my attempt to change the topic.

"Yeah, I swear I heard Coach Kate say that you were back on the court," Jessica chimes in from the backseat. "It sounded like she got a phone call from Martie."

"So, does this mean you're joining us tonight?" Missy asks, stopping at the entrance to the complex. She pulls her dad's Mercedes GL550 out onto a winding road. (It's the only car that was large enough to fit the seven of us.)

"Nope. I'm still not going," I say, unwrapping my hair

band from my ponytail. I flip my head upside down and rub out my hair.

"Did I miss something? Like when you got hit in the head with a softball?" Missy asks, inching up in her seat to check her reflection in the rearview mirror. She pouts her lips. "Because you're acting like a crazy person."

"You know she's right!" Hannah pipes up. She's sitting in the middle next to Taylor and Tamika.

"I second that," Tamika says. "You have to go. You're back on the court."

"And you're our date," Eva adds. She sits in the backseat with Jessica.

Ugh, date. I feel my stomach flip-flop thinking about Zachary arm in arm with some random girl. Then it hits me. "Wait. What are you talking about?"

"We're going as a team this year. Didn't Missy tell you? We're meeting our dates at the prom," Jessica explains.

"What?" I ask, feeling my eyes tear up. "Really, guys, don't do all that for me. I'm not going."

Missy adjusts her oversized sunglasses. "Why would the guest of honor miss the big party?" She points to my trophy. "You're going to be the first B-Dub student to collect a trophy and crown on the same day."

She squeezes my leg.

"We'll be there with you, Ky," Taylor says.

I look around at my teammates (plus Hannah) and think

about how they're the ones who've been there for me through thick and thin. "Okay, I'll go."

The girls cheer. Their voices are almost as loud as they were at the game.

"But one condition," I say, interrupting their excitement.

"Name it," Missy replies.

"Amber gets to come with us in our limo."

"Amber?" Tamika asks, disbelievingly.

"Yes, Amber." I pause. "And her friend Danielle if she wants to join."

"Are you sure?" Eva asks.

"Absolutely."

"Is the future prom princess ready?" Missy opens the door to her bedroom to find me standing there, staring at myself in her mirror, still in my bathrobe. The only indication that I'm about to leave for the prom is my hair—at Missy's insistence, it's been done into a messy updo with intertwined lavender ribbons. Other than that, I'm a total mess. I can feel Missy shaking her head behind me.

"So, are you planning on not getting dressed? Guess they're going to have to crown me instead . . ."

I'm jolted awake at the mention of a crown. "Never—" I begin to say. Then I catch sight of Missy in the mirror. "Miss, you look amazing!" Her short pale pink dress sparkles and her blonde hair is done in long, loose curls. The effect is radiant—she looks like Taylor Swift without a guitar.

"You're going to miss the pictures!" she exclaims. "Everyone's waiting! Including your dad. *And* Amber. Get dressed!"

"I just can't, Miss. It's wrong. The dress, I mean." There's a reason why I've been staring at myself instead of being productive—my mother's absence still stings. There's no way I can bring myself to wear the dress she shipped.

Missy grins. "Fortunately, you have another option." She scampers over to her walk-in closet and swings open the doors. A yellow garment bag hangs there, amid all of her Free People and Marc Jacobs. Big block letters spell out BANANA FAD.

Missy pulls the bag out of the closet. She unzips it to reveal a breathtaking lavender dress. She holds it up by the hanger and the soft material cascades down to the floor.

My mouth hangs open.

"So, I assume the dress is up to par. . . ." Missy winks.

"Wow . . . Miss. I love it!" I shout. "The way the straps loop together in the back. They almost look like two upside-down As . . . Wow." I'm speechless.

"I knew it'd be up your alley." She hangs the dress on the closet door.

"But when did you even have time to work on it?"

"You know, whenever you thought I was hanging out with Hannah." She fluffs her hair. "I can't get into college on good looks alone."

"Missy, I had no idea. You *are* really talented. And not just at marketing," I say, still staring at the dress. "You never needed to pretend like you weren't."

"It was still helpful to learn from Hannah," she concedes, shrugging. Then she shifts gears. "So, the big question is, are you going to wear it?"

"Ohmigod, yes!" I beam.

"Great! See you downstairs in five." She sashays past me and out the door.

I grab the dress off the closet door and hold it up in front of me, staring at myself in the mirror. I picture what it will be like to walk into prom, arm in arm with my friends, in a Banana Fad dress. It's not the image I originally had in mind—me holding Zachary's hand, in a dress I picked out with my mom—but surprisingly, it's even better.

My cell phone buzzes, but for once in my life, I ignore it. Everyone who cares about me is right here.

forty-three

"We're almost ready to announce this year's prom royalty!" Ms. Sealer shouts over the microphone. She then motions for the music to resume, and the girls and I return to dancing. With the exception of our brief pause during Ms. Sealer's announcement, we haven't stopped moving ever since we arrived at the Beachwood Country Club. Not even to eat.

I'm so caught up in the moment that I hardly hear Coach Kate's voice over the club mix. (The music is courtesy of Eva's boyfriend, DJ Buzz Cut Cali.)

"Kylie!" she calls out.

I dance to the music.

"Kylie!" she calls again.

Finally, I hear her. "Coach Kate!" I exclaim. "What are you doing here?" I ask. I'm shocked to see her there. And in anything but her coaching gear.

"Ms. Sealer asked me to chaperone at the last minute," she explains. She shifts around uncomfortably in her gown.

"And I thought it was a crazy day for me! You must be so tired after everything."

"No kidding. I am. I can't wait to get out of these heels." She lifts up her gown to show me the heels beneath.

"Ha ha ha," I laugh. "I know the feeling." I hear someone yell in excitement and glance back at my friends. They are still tearing it up on the dance floor.

"Kylie, I hate to interrupt you while you're clearly having such a good time. But . . ." She pauses. "I have some news."

My heart stops. It doesn't take a genius to figure out what she means by that. "Am I back off the court?" I ask. "It's okay if I am. I knew it was too much to hope for that we'd win the game and everything would be okay—"

Coach cuts me off. "No, no. It's nothing like that. I just came over to tell you that after your performance today, I got a few phone calls."

"Phone calls?"

"Yes, from some college coaches who'd like to discuss recruitment options with you."

"Really!" I exclaim. Before I can stop myself, the words come tumbling out. "Did the coach from UCLA call?!"

Coach Kate looks confused. "No, not exactly."

"Oh. Then who did?"

"A couple Division III coaches. Ithaca and Claremont."

So, not UCLA. I debate what to say to that. Then it dawns on me. "Wait, they really want me?"

"It looks that way!" Coach Kate grins.

Just then I hear Ms. Sealer clearing her throat into the microphone. I glance in her direction.

"You know what, Kylie? Let's talk about this more on Monday. Tonight is your night." Coach Kate begins to walk away.

"You sure?" I ask. "I'm just so grateful for the opportunity."

She turns back to me. "I know that, Kylie. And that's why you deserve it."

Suddenly, the music stops. "Okay. We're ready to begin," Ms. Sealer announces from the podium.

My heart skips a beat. A hush falls over the crowd, and I go to thank Coach Kate one last time. But when I look around for her, she's already gone.

"I'm going to begin by announcing the members of the court, one by one," Ms. Sealer explains. "Missy Adams."

I whistle as Missy, the picture of prom perfection, steps out onto the stage.

"Brooke Lauder," Ms. Sealer yells.

Brooke makes her way to the stage. In a sea of expertly attired guests, her gold dress still manages to dazzle.

Finally, Ms. Sealer arrives at me. "Kylie Collins," she shouts.

I meander through the crowd and step onto the dais. Then I turn around and scan the room.

"Andrew Mason," Ms. Sealer announces.

Andrew finds his spot behind Missy.

I catch sight of Zachary. He's standing near Amber, clearly

trying to get a rise out of me. In all the hoopla, I almost forgot that I'd have to deal with him tonight.

"Matt Moore."

Matt moseys up onto the stage and stands behind Brooke. Taylor cheers.

I glare at Zachary. Only one more announcement to go until I'm within a five-foot radius of him.

"Zachary Murphy."

Chants of "Murph! Murph! Murph!" erupt. The boys' basketball team leads the cheering.

Zachary finds a spot behind me onstage. He leans into me. "Where were you tonight?"

"What are you talking about?"

"I went to the guesthouse to pick you up. But you weren't there. And you didn't answer any of my calls."

"Why would I?"

"I thought you were gonna be my date."

"What!?" I have to stop myself from screaming. "What made you think that?"

"You never said no."

"Are you kidding me? My saying that I never wanted to speak to you again wasn't clear enough?"

"Eh. I've learned to ignore you when you get like that." He whispers in my ear, "No matter what, you still love me."

I move as far away from him as I can without attracting attention. "No, actually, I don't." I look around at the expectant crowd.

"Well, it wasn't like you had anyone else to go with."

"I went with my friends." Suddenly, an epiphany strikes. "Wait. How did you know that no one else invited me?"

I look back at Zachary. He's green.

"I . . . uh, didn't."

"You did."

"Believe whatever you want."

"Did you tell people not to?"

"Um . . . I—"

I stop him before he can attempt to weasel his way out. "Did you tell Brett Davidson?"

The makeshift drums sound, heralding Ms. Sealer's upcoming announcement.

Zachary regains his footing. "So what if I did?"

"Are you serious?"

"This year's prom princess and prince are . . ." Ms. Sealer squeezes her note card.

There's a long pause. I force myself to focus.

"Kylie . . ." Zachary taps me on the shoulder.

"Shut up."

"Kylie Collins and Zachary Murphy!" Ms. Sealer announces.

What?!

"See, we belong together."

"No, Zachary. We don't."

In a huff, I grab the crown from Ms. Sealer, pull Missy along, and walk off the stage.

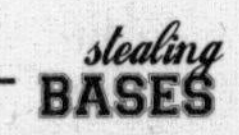

"Goodbye, Zachary," I mouth.

He attempts to grab my hand.

"I don't think you heard me. Goodbye, Zachary," I say, louder this time.

I push my way through the crowd, leaving Zachary in my dust as I go to rejoin my friends. I don't look back, but I suspect the expression on his face is one of total, complete shock. I take a moment to let it all sink in—I just won prom princess and told off Zachary Murphy. Coolly and calmly. It feels good.

A chorus of "congrats!" echoes out among the crowd. Emily, Nyla, and a bunch of the other girls from softball wave to me. Phoenix gives me a huge smile.

I wave back and mouth a big "thanks."

Finally, I reach my basketball buds. "Come on!" I exclaim. "Didn't you hear? I'm your new princess. I make the law. And I say it's time to dance!" I motion for the girls to follow me back in the direction of the stage.

The girls scurry behind me, baffled expressions on their faces. We pass Amber and some of the girls I just waved at, and I pull them along too.

I grab Eva from the line forming behind me, whispering to her to go tell her boyfriend to play *So What?* by Pink.

Then the girls and I reach our destination: the dais.

"Um . . . we don't belong up there," Amber says.

"Of course you do," I reply. I pull them onto the stage with me.

Pink's lyrics scream out just like I planned.

"It's party time!" Missy calls out. She pulls Brooke and Phoenix into the fray, and for once, I don't feel like they're out to get me. Phoenix even manages to mouth me a "congrats."

I notice Ms. Sealer slowly backing away from the dais. At this point, the stage is literally overrun with my friends. All of whom are dancing up a storm.

I snatch the crown off my head and place it on Amber's. She glows, her smile suggesting that this is the best gift anyone's ever given her. Then she passes it to Jessica, who tries it on for size. Jessica, in turn, gives it to Taylor. Who gives it to Eva. And so on.

By the time DJ Cali plays "We Are the Champions" especially for the softball team, the crown has made its way around the entire group.

And in that moment, I, Kylie Elizabeth Collins, finally let it all go.

acknowledgments

Thank you to Jane Schonberger and everyone at Pretty Tough Inc. for your support, generosity, vision, and expertise. I'm extremely proud and honored to write for the Pretty Tough brand. Thanks bunches to Ben Schrank and the über-talented gang at Razorbill for working so hard on *Stealing Bases*. A special thanks and a carton of Diet Coke goes out to the talented Gillian Levinson for your amazing editorial eye, career guidance, and patience. And last, but certainly not least, thank you to Michelle Grajkowski, my fairy agent and friend. I count my blessings every day that I'm surrounded by such an amazing team.

Thank you to my writing buds, especially the Kid Lit Authors Club and NJRWA, for your mentorship and advice. An enormous thanks goes out to Cyn Balog for talking me off the ledge, answering my bazillion questions, and your friendship. And thanks to Lauren Lesser for your honest first reads. You guys rock.

Thanks bunches to my former teammates who serve as my inspiration. And thanks to Kate Ormsby (Coach Kate) for permission to use her name as a shout-out to the Shade.

A special thanks to my teacher buds and students with an extra hug to Mike, Melanie, Sandy, Julie, Joyce, and Team Imagination for consistently picking up my slack and cheering me on. Also, thanks to the California Interscholastic Athletic Association for answering my questions and sending me research materials.

A super-duper special thanks to my family. Especially, my mom and dad for spreading the word about my books and believing in me since birth. Also, thanks to Ron, Ida, Kelly, Michael, Nicole, and Anthony for always being there whenever I needed you. Thanks to Sydney and Sabrina for forcing me to take breaks and have fun. And thanks to Kaci Olivia for giving me the courage to write, wanting to take *Head Games* into school for show-and-tell, and most of all, for just being your incredible authentic self. I love you guys.

Thank you to the librarians, booksellers, book bloggers, and readers who support the series. Your emails, messages, interviews, reviews, and blog posts mean more to me than you can ever imagine.

Stealing Bases would not be possible without the endless, unyielding support (which includes, but is not limited to, picking up groceries, running errands, and cooking dinners) from my amazing hubby, Justin. I love you!